A Candlelight Ecstasy Romance®

"FACE IT, LYNN. YOU NEED ME. IF IT WEREN'T FOR ME—"

"Oh, I need you, do I? Right, and I also need termites, hives, and a bad cold. Sure, things would be different here if it weren't for you. I wouldn't be breaking my back trying to please someone who isn't happy unless every single thing is done his way!"

"*My* way? For three months, I've practically had to bring bodyguards in every time I wanted to change the least little—"

"Yes, your way!" Lynn bellowed. "You never compromise. Nothing satisfies you, Reed."

"*You* accuse *me* of not compromising? Lynn the unbendable?"

"That's your faultless memory at work again. You were just telling me how flexible I've become. Well, those days are over. It's time you learned you can't charm me into doing whatever you want. Gull House is my restaurant, and like it or not, we're going to do things *my* way."

CANDLELIGHT ECSTASY ROMANCES®

306 ANOTHER SUNNY DAY, *Kathy Clark*
307 OFF LIMITS, *Sheila Paulos*
308 THRILL OF THE CHASE, *Donna Kimel Vitek*
309 DELICATE DIMENSIONS, *Dorothy Ann Bernard*
310 HONEYMOON, *Anna Hudson*
311 LOST LETTERS, *Carol Norris*
312 APPLE OF MY EYE, *Carla Neggers*
313 PRIDE AND JOY, *Cathie Linz*
314 STAR-CROSSED, *Sara Jennings*
315 TWICE THE LOVING, *Megan Lane*
316 MISTAKEN IMAGE, *Alexis Hill Jordan*
317 A NOVEL AFFAIR, *Barbara Andrews*
318 A MATTER OF STYLE, *Alison Tyler*
319 MAGIC TOUCH, *Linda Vail*
320 FOREVER AFTER, *Lori Copeland*
321 GENTLE PROTECTOR, *Linda Randall Wisdom*
322 SKY GYPSY, *Natalie Stone*
323 TWO SEPARATE LIVES, *Tate McKenna*
324 ENCORE OF DESIRE, *Jan Stuart*
325 WHERE LOVE MAY LEAD, *Eleanor Woods*
326 MORE PRECIOUS THAN GOLD, *Cindy Victor*
327 A DISTANT SUMMER, *Karen Whittenburg*
328 FRIENDS AND LOVERS, *Emily Elliott*
329 LOVING PERSUASION, *Emma Bennett*
330 A GLIMPSE OF PARADISE, *Cathie Linz*
331 WITH EACH CARESS, *Anne Silverlock*
332 JUST A KISS AWAY, *JoAnna Brandon*
333 WHEN MIDNIGHT COMES, *Edith Delatush*
334 MORE THAN A DREAM, *Lynn Patrick*
335 HOLD CLOSE THE MEMORY, *Heather Graham*
336 A VISION OF LOVE, *Melanie Catley*
337 DIAMOND IN THE ROUGH, *Joan Grove*

NO RESERVATIONS

Molly Katz

A CANDLELIGHT ECSTASY ROMANCE®

Published by
Dell Publishing Co., Inc.
1 Dag Hammarskjold Plaza
New York, New York 10017

ISBN: 0-440-16080-4

Printed in the United States of America

First printing—June 1985

For Bill, still the one

To Our Readers:

We have been delighted with your enthusiastic response to Candlelight Ecstasy Romances®, and we thank you for the interest you have shown in this exciting series.

In the upcoming months we will continue to present the distinctive sensuous love stories you have come to expect only from Ecstasy. We look forward to bringing you many more books from your favorite authors and also the very finest work from new authors of contemporary romantic fiction.

As always, we are striving to present the unique, absorbing love stories that you enjoy most—books that are more than ordinary romance. Your suggestions and comments are always welcome. Please write to us at the address below.

Sincerely,

The Editors
Candlelight Romances
1 Dag Hammarskjold Plaza
New York, New York 10017

CHAPTER ONE

The softshell crabs slid out of her fingers as she was transferring them from basket to sink and fell to the floor. Bending to grab them, she slipped on the patch of wetness they'd made and landed mooselike on the base of her spine.

"Uh—Lynn?" Her sister Barrie stood in the doorway of the restaurant kitchen. "I'd like you to come out and meet an applicant. That is, if you're finished resting."

Lynn glared at her petite blond twin. "Do you have to make sarcastic comments while I'm sitting here in a pool of crab juice? Now I need to change again. I smell like the inside of a hip boot. The guy will just have to cool his heels in your office for a few minutes. Here, give me a hand up, will you?"

"I'll be glad to," rumbled a distinctly unfeminine voice. Its owner, a tall man in his midthirties, stepped out from behind the doorway in back of Barrie, grasped Lynn under the arms, and hefted her to her feet. Then he collected the crabs from the floor and put them in the sink, his intrepid handling of them bespeaking a familiarity with the slimy little beasts.

"Thanks," Lynn said faintly. Humiliation burned; what a disgusting way to meet someone she had to interview! How could she sit with this man now and carry on a businesslike conversation?

Barrie looked chagrined too; she obviously had thought the man was still safely back in her office. "Lynn, this is Reed Graham; Mr. Graham, my sister, Lynn Blackburn," she said, trying to put the situation back on a dignified track.

The man turned from the sink, where he'd been washing his hands. Lynn really looked at him for the first time. His thick straight hair was the color of chestnuts; dark green eyes regarded her from behind tortoiseshell glasses. Wait—now they were lighter. Mossy, kind of, with gold glints . . .

"Nice to meet you," he said, and she broke off her trancelike perusal with a start.

"My pleasure," she answered. *I mean that,* she thought, jolted.

Barrie ahemmed from the doorway. "I have to check some supplies in the dining room, so you and Mr. Graham can talk in my office," she said, and left quickly. Lynn fought down a crazy urge to leave with her. For some reason she seemed to be having trouble catching her breath.

"Are you the present chef?" he asked Lynn.

"Oh, no," she said, brushing off her floor-length skirt as best she could. The kitchen staff was beginning to arrive; she could hear the salad and pastry chefs outside the back door, which she'd propped open to let in the May breeze with its promising kiss of mildness.

"I was washing the crabs while I had a spare minute, since they'd just come in," she explained, leading him down the hall, away from the kitchen. She felt the need to keep talking. Every time she stopped, or looked at him, that breathlessness returned. "I don't work in the kitchen at all. I do the hostessing and handle the menu, and my sister does most of the managing."

He followed her into Barrie's office, a large many-windowed room with burgundy carpeting and an eclectic mix of wood and upholstered furniture. Sunlight streamed through snowy curtains, warming the room.

Lynn motioned him to a flowered loveseat and took a wooden chair, arranging her dress so the smelly part wouldn't touch anything. She'd brought him in here intending to conduct a regulation businesslike interview. She'd hoped that would quiet her nerves, ease the awkwardness of having been found on her fanny reeking of crab by this man who was having quite a jangling effect on her. But instead she was growing more agitated; his position on the loveseat, a semirecline that was relaxed but still polite, displayed his long, solid build in a way that was impossible to ignore. His parted thighs were tree trunks encased in tawny corduroy; his torso showed thick muscles beneath his shirt, leading up to mammoth shoulders.

Lynn made herself look away—out the window, at a cobweb on the ceiling, anywhere but at this chef applicant with whom she was supposed to seem detached and efficient, but who exuded sexiness with every move, every word.

"Tell me about your experience," she choked out, her gaze following a tiny black ant along the baseboard.

He took off his glasses and put them on the loveseat arm. "Well," he said, sitting forward and brushing his hair back with a big hand, "I started out—" He stopped as they heard a knock.

"Come in," Lynn called.

A waitress opened the door and leaned inside. "They need you in the kitchen, Lynn," she said. "One of the vendors sent pollock that Roger says isn't fresh enough, and the driver's refusing to take it back."

"Barrie can handle that," Lynn said. "She's in the dining room."

"No, she isn't. The ice people called, and she had to run over there to sign our purchase order."

Lynn sighed. By now this man must think her elevator didn't stop at all floors. First she'd been found sitting in a puddle in a hostess gown, a veritable still-life-with-crabs. Then she'd spent the last few minutes trying as hard to avoid looking at him as if he were Lon Chaney. Now she'd have to end his job interview before it had begun.

"I'm sorry," she told him, rising. "I'd bring you a sherry and ask you to wait, but you know how messy these vendor battles can be. It will probably take quite a while, and then I'll be busy with the lunch crowd. Would you mind very much coming back tomorrow morning?"

"Not at all," he said, getting out of the loveseat. He stood there, making no move to go. He was looking straight into her eyes as if to pin her there; then, daringly, he let his gaze travel along her slender form, taking in the plump bosom provocatively displayed by her lavender cotton gown, the hidden legs that he'd seen in winter-creamy flashes as she'd tried to arrange her damp skirt, then up to ebony curls that fell just to her shoulders, and finally to the wide-set brown eyes that radiated warmth.

"What time will you be in?" he asked, his tone personal, intimate.

Lynn clenched her fists. She could feel that breathlessness coming back. *Keep your shoes on,* she told herself fiercely. *We're discussing a job interview, not a moonlight cruise.*

"Nine thirty," she said curtly, determined to break his spell.

"Good." He smiled, an incandescent burst that could have melted glass. "I'll be here on the dot."

He left the office and she sank with relief into the loveseat. It was still warm from him, and she took pleasure in the faint heat, enjoying the comfort of another body without the tension of having to deal with the person inside it.

What was going on? Where had her unruffled self gone, that imperturbable, conventional woman from whom sparkling green eyes over a rock-solid body would draw no livelier response than a yawn? She'd always prided herself on her ability to run her personal life from the headquarters that sat above her neck. And now—what? She didn't know, but her nerves were in an uproar. The command post seemed to be shifting.

She heard raised voices from the kitchen, yanked herself back to reality, and hurried out to tackle the fish problem.

Half an hour later, the pollock exchanged for some fresher monkfish, Lynn finally had time to run upstairs and change. Her dressing room and office were on the second floor of the white clapboard Colonial she and Barrie had converted into the luxury seafood restaurant called Gull House.

She put her fishy dress in to soak, changed into a silky black jumpsuit, and started back downstairs. There was a little time left before the lunch rush. She'd use it to work on the menu.

But from the stairs she saw Barrie in the reception area below, strolling about with elaborate casualness. Nothing could have told Lynn more clearly that her sister was waiting to pounce. Oh, well—might as well get it over with. And damned if she couldn't guess what was on Barrie's weasely little meddling mind.

Sure enough, as she reached the bottom, Barrie pretended to spot her with surprise. "Come into my parlor," she said, linking arms with Lynn and leading her firmly into the office. "What did you think of Reed Graham?" She flopped into the loveseat and hooked a denimed leg over its arm.

Lynn sat in the wooden chair. "I didn't have a chance to think anything. There was a hassle with the fish vendor that I knew would take time, so I told him to come back tomorrow."

Barrie grinned. "And?"

"And what?" She got up and began to pace the thick carpet. "Forget it. He interests me not at all. The whole idea puts me to sleep."

"So why are you pacing around like a panther in a phone booth?"

Lynn dropped into the loveseat beside her. "Because he interests me a lot."

Barrie clapped in glee. "I knew it! Isn't he delicious?"

"Don't get excited. I'm not going to do anything about it."

"Lynn! Why on earth not?"

"For the same reason I keep telling you to cut this out. I don't want to get seriously involved with a man until I have my worklife together."

"I can't see why not. You've had some great relationships. I'll never understand why you broke your engagement to Don."

Lynn gritted her teeth, irritated by her sister's persistence. "You know why. Because I knew that if I married Don it would be too easy to simply stop working and start a family—and then I'd never have resolved the work thing, never have found out what I can really do."

Barrie gazed at her with the limpid brown eyes that were their only common characteristic. "But *I'm* happy being married and working."

"That's because your work makes you happy in the

first place," Lynn said tightly. They'd had versions of this conversation often. Would Barrie never understand?

"So why did we hock our vital organs to buy this place? I know you love Gull House as much as I do, Lynn."

"I do love it. I just don't love what I'm doing in it." Barried started to interrupt, but Lynn pushed on. "I know, we divided up the work so we could each do what we were good at. I should feel fine. We dreamed of owning a landmark restaurant. How can I be unsatisfied when we've made that dream come true? I don't know what the trouble is, but it's there."

"Well," Barrie said, "if we can get back to business—"

"You mean, if I'm willing to pretend your unforgivable intrusion into my private life never occurred—"

"Intrusion? No way!" Barrie said, matching Lynn's grin. "Where would you be without my 'intrusions'? Eating tuna out of a can and playing Scrabble with your hamster."

"I don't have a hamster."

"You'll be buying one any day now, you twenty-nine-year-old spinster. Hey, spinster with a hamster. I like that."

"Has a ring to it," Lynn said dryly, getting up.

"Of course, if you had a mister, you wouldn't be a spinster, and you wouldn't need the hamster," Barrie said, laughing. "Must you go? I was just warming up."

"That's what I'm afraid of," Lynn said. She opened the door.

"By the way," Barrie tossed over her shoulder, "I'll probably hire him."

Lynn banged the door shut and whirled around, glaring.

"Easy, Lynn. He's definitely the cream of the crop. The green eyes have nothing to do with it. His experience is so impressive. He's worked all over the country. This will be his first shot at New England cuisine, but I'm sure he can handle it."

"Don't I get a vote?"

"No more than I do on food. You know personnel is my turf," Barrie reminded her kindly.

Lynn looked her sister in the eye. "You're trying to force him on me."

"I sure am. But even if you insist on keeping your libido packed away in the attic with mothballs, he's still the best chef I've interviewed—and Roger has to leave in a month. He'd like to go a lot sooner, if we can get a replacement on deck."

Lynn leaned against the closed door and folded her arms. "I don't want him."

"Uncross your toes and say that."

"Oh, stop it, Barrie!" she snapped. "I'm sure there are other possibles. You've seen several people, there are more to come—"

"Not many, and no one who looks promising. This is the lousiest crop of applicants, and Graham shines. We should grab him. He's only in Maine for a few days; if we don't hire him, he'll go back to his New York job."

"New York?"

"See what I mean?" Barrie went to Lynn, made a valiant attempt to sling an affectionate arm around her half-a-head-taller sister. "We should snap him up. How often do we get a chance—"

"No!" Lynn shouted, wrenching away. "I don't want him here, and that's the end of it!" She yanked the door open and stalked out, immediately coming face to face with Reed.

"What the hell are you doing here?" she shouted.

Reed jumped back as if she'd breathed flame. Two waitresses filling vases in the dining room spun around.

Anger and embarrassment heated her cheeks. "Sorry," she muttered.

"I came back for my glasses. I must have left them in the office," Reed said defensively.

Her senses reeled. During the few seconds they'd been close she'd been hit by an overwhelming mingling of scents—his own, unadulterated by after-shave, a joyous blend of freshly shampooed hair, sweet skin, the hint of an active male body. Electricity seemed to flow from him in a palpable stream, curling around and behind her, pulling her nearer. She noticed the suggestion of a beard. For a mad moment she wanted to stroke it, feel the roughness of his chin, imagine what it would be like against . . .

"Well," she spat out, involuntarily groping to maintain her outrage, to mask his effect on her, "what are you standing here for? Go in and look for them!"

His face darkened. The battle in his mind was revealed in the shifting of his features. It was as if she were watching a television screen. Part of him yearned to tell her to jump in the Atlantic; a sensible side remembered that a job was at stake.

The less practical side won. "You," he thundered, pointing a long finger at her, "have crummy manners, a rotten disposition, and a lot of gall! I could have done plenty for this restaurant. You would have been lucky to have me. Now I wouldn't work here if it was a choice between Gull House and McDonald's!" He pulled open the front door and stomped out, slamming it behind him.

The dinner rush was over. Lynn stood in the doorway to the dining room, watching the few remaining customers. It had been an easy night, all things considered. The encounter with that new applicant for the chef's job had left an uneasy feeling that lingered—she'd been unreasonably rude, probably partly in reaction to Barrie's meddling; the poor man had gotten an undeserved earful, and she regretted losing her temper. Still, it was just as well. The last thing she needed right now was a chef who turned her joints to marshmallow fluff.

The phone rang. "Gull House, can I help you?" she answered automatically. Probably a reservation for tomorrow.

"Is this Lynn?" a male voice asked, the newly familiar resonance sending an odd liquid heat through her.

"Yes," she said hoarsely.

"Thought I'd give you a chance to apologize."

"Who is this?" she asked unnecessarily, ashamed of herself.

He simply waited.

She smiled. Hunks one, brats nothing. "I'll take that chance. You're right, I—"

"An apology can't be conveyed by the voice alone," he interrupted. "I'd like to know you're truly sorry. I can only be sure if I see your eyes. You'll be finished there in—what, an hour?"

"About that, but—"

"Fine. I'll meet you outside." He hung up before she could utter another syllable.

Nearly sixty minutes later everyone else had gone and she sat in the reception area, alone. She'd checked, rechecked, and triple-checked the dining room for tomorrow. The dishes of matches and mints near her had not only been filled but their contents arranged in patterns that would have pleased Picasso.

She gazed around the reception area. Its peaceful beauty was a balm to her tortured emotions. The dusty-mauve carpet was cushiony under the mahogany chairs and end tables; silvery curtains fell in soft folds, framing windows that showed a sprinkling of stars on blue-black.

With nothing left to do, she had to recognize why she was still there. She propped her feet on a chair that didn't look sturdy enough to be breathed on heavily, checked her watch and tried vainly to relax. After the call, she'd intended to just finish up and leave; since he hadn't waited for an answer, she couldn't be blamed if she didn't stay. But she'd watched herself drag out her small tasks to excruciating slowness. She had to admit now that she'd been trying to let the decision make itself by default.

Why, though? Why hadn't she simply left?

For the same reason your heart just went into overdrive, she acknowledged wryly as she heard the soft toot of his horn.

She went out and locked up. He'd parked in the circular drive and was leaning against the car, watching her.

Didn't he ever do anything but *lounge?* Lynn thought as she stood on the steps. That semirecline was so annoying! It thrust his lower torso forward in a way that was . . . well, just annoying. The outside lights were off and she couldn't see his face, but she'd bet that smile was there, that brilliant, glowing, annoying . . .

"Nice place you've got," he drawled in the darkness.

"Thanks," she said weakly.

"Bet you don't ever really see it anymore," he said. "Come on down here and look with me."

She joined him by the car. This close, she could see his face, and he was eyeing her expectantly; he seemed to want her to lean against the car with him.

"Go ahead," he said as she eased back hesitantly. "You won't get dirty. I just rented the car yesterday. It's clean." He stepped in front of her and gently shifted her shoulders and positioned her arms so that her weight was supported properly. For a moment he forgot to take his hands away, and they rested on her arms, the fingers loose, brushing. Heat radiated from his eyes to hers in the blackness. He leaned nearer, and she felt an invisible something pulling, tugging . . . but then he seemed to remember himself, and he stepped back.

Lynn shook off the net of sensation before it could envelop her entirely. She forced her voice to a light cheeriness.

"You know, this *is* comfortable," she said.

He moved back to his spot beside her and she felt a jab of disappointment. His hands had been touches of flame, and a part of her that got failing grades in Behaving Intelligently, the part that kept her walking around the dining room like an automaton when she could have finished up fast and avoided him, missed their enticing warmth.

"Beautiful, isn't it?" he whispered.

She was so exquisitely conscious of the press of his arm at her side, his scent, the aura his bigness created, that she could barely concentrate. She willed herself to really look at Gull House, study it, see it as he did.

"It is beautiful," she said. "I haven't looked at it this way in years."

They fell silent, gazing at the stately white house with its gleaming black shutters and carved windowboxes. In the inky night it seemed to glow. Lynn inhaled deeply, savoring the sea air with its salty bite, adjusting her ears to pick up the muted hiss that was all that could be heard of the ocean several blocks away as the breakers crashed.

"One thing I'd like to do," he said softly.

"Yes?" She held her breath.

"Look for my glasses."

She slumped against the car, simultaneously disappointed and relieved. The fierce tingling in her flesh, which had begun just before she'd found out what it was he wanted to do, was suddenly gone—and she was giggling. She couldn't help it—the situation was so ridiculous. Here she'd been in the moonlight, tensely awaiting the suggestion this gorgeous man was about to whisper, agonizing over how to handle it—and all he wanted was to find his glasses. She laughed harder, almost doubling over.

"Did I miss a punch line?" he asked.

"No," she managed. "You gave it!"

He waited patiently for her to collect herself. "I'm glad you think I'm a funny guy," he said when her chortles had died away, "but usually I *know* when I've made a joke, and unless I've gone senile in the last few minutes . . ."

"No, no," she said, dabbing at her streaming eyes with her fingers. "I was being silly. Don't take it personally. It's been a long day."

"For me too." He leaned close and smiled at her. "In fact, this isn't my first lesson in not taking things personally from you."

He was right. All he'd done was apply for a job, and she'd put him through the mill.

"The least I can do is help you find your glasses," Lynn said, fishing in her handbag for her keys. "They're probably in my sister's office. Let's try there first."

He followed her up the steps, waited while she

opened the door. They went into Barrie's office and she snapped on the light. "Where were you sitting?" she asked, as if she hadn't seen his ghost lounging in the loveseat all day.

He pointed. "In that wooden chair."

She looked sharply at him.

"Just testing," he said, grinning easily.

She wished she could crawl into a desk drawer. The man's ability to embarrass her was never-ending.

He was feeling around in the upholstery. Glad for the distraction, Lynn joined him.

"Here they—oops!" he said. Yanking the glasses too zealously from the loveseat innards, he had broken off an earpiece. Sheepishly he tucked the two parts into his shirt pocket. "See what you do to me? I was so busy looking at you, I wasn't paying attention."

Lynn stood rooted to the floor, trapped by his smoky gaze. Those eyes, that power . . . it would devour her if she let it.

She looked at a point next to his shoulder. "You need some consolation. How about a cup of coffee?" she said.

"I was going to take you out for coffee."

"That's nice, but why go to a restaurant? We're *in* a restaurant."

"You're all shut down for the night . . ."

"No problem. I could use some myself. Follow me."

She led him into the dark dining room. The reception room light cast a dim glow that was enough to navigate by. Threading her way among the pristinely set tables, she went to a small one in a corner. She pulled out a chair, urged him to sit, lit the candle in its brass holder. The flame bounced off the metal, setting his maybe-green-maybe-gold eyes alight with sparks. He watched her every move.

Shushing the voice that kept demanding to know what she thought she was doing reopening the restaurant at midnight, she hurried to the kitchen, stopping to grab two bottles from the bar.

Ten minutes later she was back with a tray that held some apple-leaf pastries and two sugar-rimmed stemmed glasses of brandy-and-tequila-laced coffee, which she flamed with the candle.

"See?" she couldn't resist saying smugly as he sipped with obvious pleasure. "I *can* function in the kitchen and stay on my feet."

He reached beneath the table and knocked on its leg.

"If you were aiming for my knee, you missed," she told him.

"If you were aiming to scare me away, *you* missed."

She looked up at him in the candlelight, confused.

He put down his pastry. "I heard you tell your sister you don't want me here."

She turned away, shamed. It was becoming a familiar feeling.

"I don't imagine you usually go around treating people the way you did me this morning. Anybody who's this gracious"—he held up the fragrant coffee—"can't be as difficult as you tried to seem. What does that say to you?"

"Does it matter? I think I'm about to hear what it says to *you.*"

He winced. "Sorry. Don't mean to be preachy. Maybe you were trying to make me ask myself, 'Why should I work in this loonybin?' Your sister liked me fine. I thought we had a deal. Then I find this other lady who's supposed to interview me sitting on the floor with a bunch of crabs around her, and from then on everything goes to hell."

"I guess I can't blame you for seeing it that way."

"You show me another way to see it, and I'll be grateful."

Lynn sat back and sipped her coffee. His perceptions were too acute for comfort. "Isn't it my turn to ask a question?"

"I'm not sure I'm going to like this."

"I'm not sure you are either. Why would a successful New York chef want to work in a conservative seafood restaurant in Ogunquit, Maine, where the average age of the customers is ninety and the most exciting activity is watching grass grow?"

He picked up his pastry and slowly finished it. Lynn had doused the reception room light when she came back, trusting the table candle to light her way, and they sat in darkness except for the flame and the bit of moonlight spilling through the windows. It was cozy, being in their own faintly glowing corner, amid all the tables in the shadowy room, but also a little spooky. Lynn was starting to feel itchy with the silence when he answered, "You seem to be asking, 'What's the matter with you that you have to settle for a place like this?' Let me guess," he said as she started to interrupt. "You've decided I must have been involved in a scandal. They rode me out of town at sunup and . . . no? How about this? I accidentally used strychnine instead of flour in a batch of profiteroles. Twenty pillars of society went off in ambulances moaning that they should have ordered the chocolate mousse. To escape prosecution, I—"

"Mr. Graham!" she said sharply.

He lifted his luxuriant brows. "Mr. Graham? After all we've been to each other?"

"Reed," she said grudgingly. "Is it too much to expect you to simply answer my question?"

"Is it too much to expect you to simply answer mine?"

"You didn't ask one," she said, eyes innocently wide.

"Oh, I see. Unless it's one sentence with a subject and verb and a squiggle at the end, it's not a question. Okay. Why were you trying to scare me away from a job we both know I'd do beautifully?"

"How should I know you'd do it beautifully? No, honestly," she pushed on as he began to look angry in the weak light. "I know practically nothing about you. Barrie told me very little."

"Because you've got fine instincts, and they tell you I'm damn good. That much I know. What I don't know is why you're so determined not to have me here. Don't tell me it's nothing personal. It can only be personal. You don't scream 'I don't want him here!' about a candidate whose sautéeing technique isn't up to par. And you just admitted you know nothing about me."

She was silent. He had her, of course.

Arms on the table, he leaned forward. "I don't think you're repelled by me. In fact, I have the feeling you like me," he said, his eyes searching her face.

His nearness and his open, warm expression were almost irresistible. Lynn forced herself to draw back and think. She felt defensiveness rising, the antidote to the responsive chord his gently persistent questions were striking. It would be so like her to turn on him now, spit angry words, make a smokescreen out of them—to drive him off, quell this threat to her boundary fence.

But there was something different about this particular intruder: it was harder to want to chase him away. The urge was there, all right, but it was warring with an incredibly strong yen to keep him with her.

"That is the reason," she said finally, giving up, exhausted from the emotional tug of war.

"You like me? That's the reason . . ." He nodded slowly, the pieces clicking into place. "What happened with the other guy?"

"What other guy?"

"The guy who worked here that you didn't have a happy ending with."

She frowned, trying to follow. "Oh. No, there wasn't anyone. The point is, I don't want there to be. I'm trying to make some decisions about my career. The kind I don't want to be distracted from."

"By a guy."

"Right."

"Well," he said, toying with his coffee glass, "I

won't insult your intelligence by saying you have nothing to fear from me. You must know by now that I think you're special. But I can behave myself when I have to."

A tingle of pleasure ran up her spine at this first definite indication that the attraction was mutual. She cursed herself. That wasn't what she wanted to feel. Then his eyes met hers again, and she felt weak with the joy of it, the rapture of knowing he felt what she did. She wondered how it would be if those lips came closer, closer, till they were a breath away, then settled softly, sweetly, on hers . . .

"Can *you?*" he asked.

She was silent for a moment, then asked, "What do you mean, can *I?*"

"You know. Can *you* behave *your*self?"

"Can I hold back from jumping on your irresistible bones, is that what you're asking?"

"Yes," he said.

"I think I can manage."

"Then," he said, grinning wolfishly, "what are you worried about? Look, I really want to work here. It's exactly the job I'm looking for. I have a lot to contribute to Gull House. You admit your only hesitation is that you don't want to get involved with me—so if we both keep that from happening, where's the problem?"

She sighed. It was like debating with Mount Rushmore. "*Now* is it my turn?" she asked. "I answered your question. I still want to know why you're here."

"Fair enough. I come from Maine. Born in Kittery,

thirty-seven years ago. Graduated from the University of Maine, and haven't been back since. I have no family here anymore—my folks live on the West Coast and my sister's in Boston. See, I wanted to do restaurant work, but I knew I wouldn't learn enough about cuisine if I stayed in New England. So I worked around the country, starting at the bottoms of some very prestigious totem poles. I've had chef spots in San Francisco and New York. I've proved myself—and now I want to do what I love in the *place* I love. I kept looking for openings that were in my league, and when I heard the Gull House chef was leaving, I phoned and came right up."

"Well, we're in your league as far as size and reputation are concerned," Lynn said, "but—classic New England food? Won't you be bored?"

"I'm not worried," he said confidently, rising to help her clear the table. He snuffed the candle and they walked cautiously through the dining room, now lighted only by the moon. Lynn left their glasses in the kitchen and they went out.

"Can I drive you home?" Reed asked.

"No, thanks, my car's in the back," she said, reluctant to leave this man she'd used everything short of a cattle prod to get rid of earlier today.

"Let me walk you around then," he said, and touched her back to guide her as they moved along the driveway.

Funny how darkness forces people to stay close, Lynn thought, enjoying the slight pressure of his hand. "I'm surprised there isn't a population explosion in

Alaska," she said, not realizing until right afterward that she'd muttered audibly.

"Again?" he said.

"Nothing. I was, uh, just thinking that I ought to change the menu to include baked Alaska."

She unlocked her Chevette and was opening the door when he said, "I forgot something."

"It can't be your glasses," Lynn said. "That's where I came in."

"I was thinking more of something you owe me. Something you started to give me on the phone, that I said would only be valid in person."

"My apology for screaming at you."

"That's it."

"Sorry," she said, opening her car door and bending to duck inside.

He grasped her arm and pulled her back out. "Not so fast. I could have settled for that on the phone. I want to see in your eyes that you mean it."

She pursed her lips stubbornly. "There isn't enough light back here."

He took matches from his jacket pocket and struck one.

She watched it burn down. "You'll singe your fingers."

"I've got plenty more."

"You *are* special. Most people only have ten."

"I meant matches." He struck another.

"I know."

"Do I get my apology before we both die of sulfur poisoning?"

"Is there such a thing?"

"There will be if you don't quit stalling."

"Who's stalling?"

He threw down his sixth match. "Forget the apology. I think I preferred you screaming."

She laughed. "I am sorry, really. And now I have to go home."

She slid into the driver's seat, and Reed closed the door. He motioned for her to roll down the window, and when she did he slowly raised a hand and trailed a caressing finger down her cheek, barely touching, but leaving a path of fire nonetheless. Then he backed away, his eyes still on her.

Lynn started along the drive. She knew the image of him in her rearview mirror, lounging against a tree, smiling in the red glow from her taillights, would shimmer in her memory all night.

CHAPTER TWO

"I guess this means it's okay to hire him," Barrie said as Lynn came in the kitchen door. Barrie was holding up the stemmed glasses from the night before. Damn! She'd been sure she'd get in first.

"I didn't see your car," Lynn said.

"It's at the gas station. Low tire. Well?" she drawled suggestively, waving the glasses.

Lynn shook her head in resignation. "How did you figure out what I used them for?"

"We didn't come from the same embryo for nothing. I—"

"We didn't come from the same embryo at all, you ignoramus. Not even identical twins do. They come from the same egg or zygote or something," Lynn began. "But fraternal twins—"

Barrie spread her hands. "Enough. What do I know about biology? I studied psychology in college. Anyway, it was obvious that since you're usually the last one here . . . and from the look on Graham's face when you blasted him yesterday and he blasted you back, he wasn't going to leave it like that . . . I just put two and two together—"

"And got eight. How do you know I didn't have coffee with one of the staff?"

"There was also the small matter of some pastry crumbs around that cozy corner table, and a candleholder that hadn't been cleaned . . ."

"All right, Poirot, I give up," Lynn said.

"Maybe now you'll drop that nonsense about no involvements until you get your career ironed out."

"It isn't nonsense, Barrie."

"Oh, it is, too." She paced the kitchen, her single wheat-colored pigtail bouncing. Her small, shapely form was encased in a plaid flannel shirt and jeans that fit like a banana skin; she wore them so constantly that the denim had forgotten how to assume any other shape. "I don't doubt you really want to change your work routine, but it's silly to say you can't have a relationship until you do. I had a feeling you'd rethink that if the right guy came along."

"What gives you the right to pick my motives apart?" Lynn asked, exasperated.

"The fact that I'm doing this, for one thing," Barrie answered, putting the glasses in the dishwasher. "You could have done it last night, gotten rid of the evidence, and I'd never have known the guy was here. Instead you left them for me to find—"

"Just because you took a psychology course or two—"

"I have a degree in it, as you well know. And you only needle me that way when I'm hitting home. Anyway, you practically stuck them in my face, which means you're asking for my opinion, even if your conscious doesn't realize it."

Lynn was silent.

"Go ahead, deny it."

"I can't."

"Okay. Shall I continue?"

Lynn dropped her hostess dress into a chair and put her coat on top of it. "If you must."

"You've been saying that stuff for a couple of years now," Barrie went on, "about not doing one thing until the other is settled, and I think you're using it—"

"—to keep myself inert."

Barrie closed her mouth in surprise.

Lynn burst out laughing. "I'm allowed to have a perception once in a while too," she said. "You look like you've just met a talking dog. I've been thinking about this a lot. Maybe I came to some of the same conclusions you're about to bludgeon me with."

Barrie looked concerned. "Am I coming on too strong?"

"No more than usual. I chewed on this for half the night, and I guess I finally realized that if you go around saying you can't do A until you do B, that's a great excuse for never doing either. I sort of froze in place a couple of years ago when I saw that this restaurant we worked so hard to get wasn't making me happy. I was afraid to discover I'd done the wrong thing and have to get out, which would've left *you* stranded. And I didn't want the temptation of a relationship, the chance to chuck it all and have a family. I knew that if I took that escape, I'd never solve my career problem. So I just did neither."

Barrie nodded slowly in satisfaction, like a teacher watching a student finally master square roots. "So you think maybe you're ready to do both?"

"I'm not sure," Lynn said, absently rearranging a box of green peppers. "I just know that something's starting. I don't know where it's headed, but I'm going to climb on and see what happens. So—to go back to what you said first, yes, you can hire him."

"I already did."

Lynn spun around, dropping a pepper, which rolled toward Barrie. She scooped it up and threw it back to Lynn, who caught it automatically. "When?" she demanded.

"This morning. When I found exhibit A. I called his hotel and asked when he could start. Somehow he didn't seem surprised. He's going to call his boss in New York to see what they need from him, and he'll be in tonight to watch and work a little."

"You could have waited to talk to me," Lynn told her, stung.

"I should have; I know I'm being pushy. But look at it from my point of view," Barrie said. "I'm acting out of love for my two favorites—you and Gull House."

"Then you could have told me sooner, instead of letting me go on like an idiot."

"I tried to, when you came in. You were too busy demonstrating your superior knowledge of biology."

"Touché," Lynn said. "Well—so he'll be working here. Don't they need a lot of notice in New York?"

"I asked him that. They knew he was looking, and they're moving his number two up."

Lynn felt woozy. She was just beginning to absorb the reality. First she'd been up late last night, trying to hold her own in verbal Ping-Pong with Reed while strange, unfamiliar sensations took over her body, distracting her, hounding her. Then she'd rolled around in her big bed for hours, sleepless, alternately wishing she'd chased Reed off for good and happy she hadn't. Now she'd come to work, draggy from the night but glad of the morning's fresh perspective, only to find that the fates had been busy . . . *very* busy.

"Well, all I know," Lynn said, "is that it's going to be an interesting summer." Feeling Barrie's eyes following her, she took her dress and coat and went upstairs to change.

It was the peak of the dinner rush that night, busy even for a Friday, considering that the season wouldn't officially begin until late June. Lynn was moving in what she called her hostess rhythm: operating at frantic speed while appearing serenely unhurried.

"Gull House," she said into the phone cradled on her shoulder as she counted out menus for the group she was about to seat. "Seven thirty tomorrow? Sorry, I'm booked, but I can offer you six or eight thirty. . . . Spell that, please? Fine, we'll see you then."

She seated her party, noticed a waitress trying to catch her eye, and started toward her.

"That man in the kitchen they're saying is the new chef? He's asking for you," whispered Antal, a cheerful, motherly French-Canadian who was one of Lynn's favorites.

Lynn's pulse began to race. She'd managed to keep thoughts of Reed at bay by working like a demon, which hadn't been difficult on this busy night, but tucked away all day had been the warm nugget of anticipation at the prospect of seeing him again. She'd wondered what she'd say, whether they'd still have last night's rapport, and when and how she'd see him during the evening. Some nights she was in the kitchen constantly, with sendbacks and special requests, other times she was hardly there at all. She could have manufactured an excuse, of course; but that newly reawakened corner of her self, the pragmatic, survivor part that had finally admitted she was dragging her feet on getting her life moving again, found that offensive.

Now, thrown by the heady reality of Reed not a hundred feet away, asking for her, Lynn whispered back to Antal, "What should I do?"

If Antal was surprised by the change in her employer—by this efficient woman suddenly turned to custard—she didn't show it.

"Do?" Antal echoed. "There is only one thing for a woman to do when a man with this one's fire wants to see her, eh? Do not ask why or where or how. Just go." She patted Lynn's flushed cheek. "Do it. I watch things here, eh?" She hurried away, her comfortable hips moving beneath her blue uniform, and Lynn, heart pounding harder, went into the kitchen.

There he was, bent over a skillet with Roger. He

hadn't spotted her. She caught her breath, unable to resist stealing this moment to watch him before he realized she was there.

He wore a forest-green shirt, the sleeves rolled to his elbows, beneath a white apron. How did he manage to look so masculine in that thing? His thick, shiny auburn hair fell over his forehead, covering part of his glasses. As she watched, he pushed it away, in a gesture that was already becoming endearingly familiar. The snapped-off temple, she noticed, had been mended with masking tape.

Alerted by some instinct older than the world, Reed looked up, directly at her. The green of his shirt turned his eyes a brilliant jade. Immobilized by his magnetic pull, she did nothing. A smile slowly spread across his face. He bent back to Roger, spoke, pushed his hair away again, and threaded his way through the crowded, noisy kitchen to her.

For those few moments Lynn hadn't cared what planet she was on, much less who might be noticing her catatonic reaction to Reed. But now that he'd seen her and was heading her way, the spell was broken, and she glanced around to see whether she'd been observed.

"I'm right here," he said.

"I know. I was just, uh, seeing how things are going in the kitchen."

"What?" He bent closer, unable to hear over the din. She could smell his heated skin, the seductive sweetness of his breath.

"What did you want to see me about?" she asked,

her jitteriness making her voice loud in his ear, and he moved back abruptly. This wasn't going well at all.

He flashed his devastating smile. "I just wanted to say hello. I kept hoping you'd come in here, and when you didn't, I asked that great French lady to give you the word."

She couldn't help but smile back. So she hadn't been the only one on tenterhooks tonight!

"How do you like it so far?" she asked. *Wonderful, Lynn. Maybe next you can ask him if he comes here often.*

"I like it very much. I know I'll be happy here."

The graciousness that functioned on automatic pilot when necessary had deserted Lynn tonight. She racked her brain for a reply, the sensuous power of his gaze making her as incapable of carrying on this conversation as if he were speaking Urdu.

"I—um . . ." she began, desperate to insert something into the gaping hole that had suddenly opened in their exchange. "Did Roger show you where to hang your coat?" she finished inanely, wanting to hide under the freezer.

He was peering at her oddly, as if wondering whether he'd heard right, when a waitress pushed through the swinging doors, her face quivering with outrage.

"What is this?" she shouted. "Ten years this customer has been eating baked haddock every Friday. Now all of a sudden it's got some garbage on it! This lady, her digestion—"

Lynn snapped back to life. "What's the trouble, Beth?" she asked. Then the aroma reached her: onions.

"*This* is the trouble," Beth said, thrusting the dish under her nose.

Lynn took it. The fish looked the same as usual, with its golden crumb topping, but grated onion had been added to the crumbs.

"I didn't make that," Roger said in a puzzled tone at her elbow. "I don't—oh." He turned to look at Reed, who was watching them all, bewildered.

"I made it," Reed said. "What's the matter with it?"

"Nothing, if you're in New York City," Lynn answered. She forced her temper down; she couldn't stand to make a spectacle of herself again, as she had yesterday. The staff was going to get together and chip in for a straitjacket if this didn't stop. "Can we step out back for a minute?" she asked him.

He scowled but followed her outside. "Look, what's the problem? I don't get it. Do you want your customers collapsing into their plates, stone cold dead of boredom? Plain fish? You might as well bake a folded diaper and serve it."

"The baked fish has a crumb—"

"Right, a crumb topping, Roger told me. Cracker crumbs and butter. I added a little minced onion. Are you going to call the police?"

"But you shouldn't—"

"Shouldn't *what?* That waitress acted as though I danced out there in a G-string and presented the fish with its head still on. This is what you're hiring me for, you know—to make excellent food. The extra touches I have up my sleeve are your good luck."

"I admire your skill, of course, but—"

"Skill? Are you serious? Plumbers have *skill.* Dog groomers have *skill.* If you wanted *skill,* you should have hired a robot with a wire whisk. What I provide is *talent,* and if you can't appreciate—"

"Are you going to let me finish a sentence?" Lynn yelled, her control slipping. She'd tried to mollify him, but he was hell-bent on being defensive. "I appreciate you! I appreciate your talent! I'm sorry you think skill is a filthy word. I meant it as a compliment! But that customer of Beth's is a sweet lady who might be the oldest living native of the Northeast, and changing the way her fish is cooked, even with just a little onion, is a major trauma to her. Why can't I point that out without your ego getting all—"

"It's not ego! I'm the one who should ask why! Why an experienced artist with the talent to add some real flair has to raise his hand and ask permission to improve a little piece of fish. I should have known this sort of stuff would happen in the—up here," he said, pushing his hair out of his face.

"In the what?" she asked with deceptive sweetness.

"Never mind."

"Were you by any chance going to say 'in the sticks'?" she asked in the same tone.

"All right, yes, I was. But—"

"Well, let me remind you," she shouted, hands on her hips, "that the sticks didn't come looking for you! So why don't you go back to the bright lights and let us locals sit around the pickle barrel?" Without waiting for him to answer, she pounded up the steps, stalked through the kitchen, and out, ignoring the startled faces.

Antal raised a concerned eyebrow from the end of the dining room.

Lynn went to her. "Do I look as bad as I think I do?" she asked.

"Oui. Ferocious, like a bear."

Lynn ran a hand over her face, as if that would fix everything. "Will you cover the door for another minute while I run up and see what I can do?"

Antal nodded, her kind eyes sympathetic, and Lynn climbed the stairs to her dressing room, thinking wryly that it was too bad Barrie wasn't here to congratulate her on this auspicious beginning to her brave new lifestyle.

"I'm getting a little bored, having to give you chances to apologize," came Reed's voice from the shadows by the back steps, making Lynn jump as she unlocked the Chevette.

She whirled around angrily. "You scared me."

He stepped out of the darkness. Now he wore a tweed jacket over the green shirt. In the moonlight, hazed by a filmy overlay of cloud, his hair shone with amber lights.

"Would you slug me if I told you you're lovely when you're mad?" he asked.

She gave him an icy glare, which threatened to crack as she realized that by now he must think her repertoire of moods consisted of anger, anger, and anger. Then the old-movie quality of his line, delivered in a Bogart voice, began to sink in, and she laughed.

"That's better," he said, leaning against her car. "I was beginning to think that frown was permanent."

"I'm not really the one who should apologize this time."

"True. You *were* snappish—"

"But only after—"

"—I acted like a jerk."

She smiled. "First-night jitters?"

"I guess. Anyway, I'd like to make it up to you. Do you mind if we take your car?"

If she looked really carefully, which was hard to do without giving herself away, she could just make out a few reddish-brown chest hairs above his shirt.

"Take it where?" she asked foggily.

"Out for a hot fudge sundae."

She tried to look into his eyes. "Nothing's open."

"Good point. That brings me to my second suggestion. A walk on the beach."

"The beach? At this hour? In this weather? Are you crazy?"

"Yes, yes, yes, and no," he said, pulling himself away from the car. "Come on. It's not that cold, and this isn't so late for us night people."

Even in the chilly spring air, with both of them in coats, his body sent a rhythm, a warmth that drummed its way through her and caught an answering pulse. His breathing quickened; he felt it too. He reached a hand toward her, but she drew back for an instant and the thread was snapped.

Reed walked around to the passenger side. He tried the door and, when it didn't open, stood patiently until she unlocked it from the inside.

"Maine has the best coastline in the world. I used to love walking this beach," he said, folding himself into the small seat.

Lynn drove automatically, her hands making all the right moves, her body in turmoil. Her face felt heated and she rolled down the window, letting in the sea air with its salt tang, damp on her face as they neared the ocean. What a thrill to be on her way to the kind of adventure she never allowed herself, her car filled with the enticing scent of the man beside her. Most nights after work were spent at home in her robe, making cinnamon tea, maybe listening to music before going to bed. Reed's suggestion had shocked her for a moment —but only in the way cool wine is a shock on a parched throat. Recalling how she'd agonized after their fight tonight, she was delighted to find her peevish temper hadn't done much damage. The slamming finale had been mainly his fault; but so far she'd been just too negative with this man she'd known for only two days, who'd pierced her protective shell of inertia. She hated the negativism, knew it was her defense, was trying to cut it out—and was ecstatic at being with him now, instead of home alone cursing herself.

She parked by the wooden steps that led over the dunes to the beach. They went up the flight and down, Lynn moving as if in a dream. The breakers thundered; she felt the spray on her face as she stepped onto the hard sand. Clouds had moved in and the night was now so black she couldn't see anything but trawlers' lights in the distance. She hesitated, feeling she'd step into inky nothingness, but Reed walked as if he could see in the dark, pulling her along, adjusting his stride to hers.

They walked without speaking for a few minutes, and Lynn's eyes adjusted so she could see a bit. She glanced toward the waterline, but could only make out a blurred silvery glow in the froth of the waves as they broke against the sand.

Reed inhaled deeply and sighed with pleasure. "I'm so glad to be back. There's nothing anywhere like this smell, the feel of this air."

"I know. I wasn't born here, but I think people appreciate their adopted homes even more than their real ones."

"How did you happen to come here?" he asked.

"Barrie and I wanted to own a restaurant, a seafood place on the coast. You see, we went to college intending to do other things—she studied psychology and I was going to teach. We'd always been close, but we'd never considered working together. Then, when we finished school, we discovered we had the same ambition—to open a place like Gull House. We worked like mad to buy it, and for the first couple of years it was touch and go—but eventually people realized we weren't hippies selling tofuburgers. Slowly we earned a reputation for really good food, the classic kind they trust, and we feel obliged to keep giving them that. We adopted Ogunquit, and it adopted us back."

"Why the seacoast, though, exactly?"

Lynn shrugged. "We grew up in Illinois. This was exotic to us. It still feels exotic. I love it."

Rolling her words back, she realized the picture she'd sketched looked like two old pussycats sitting by the fire with their knitting.

"We're not neurotically dependent on each other or anything," she rushed to add. "Barrie's married, after all, and I—uh—"

"—have my career conflicts to keep me warm," he finished for her.

She chuckled at the crack. It was truer than he knew.

"Want to talk about that?" he asked.

"There isn't much to say. I love Gull House, but I don't love what I do there. And before you suggest it, swapping jobs with Barrie isn't the answer. She does personnel and almost all the detail work; she likes it, and she's better at it than I would ever be. And she won't go near the dining room, which is why I do the hostessing. She gets this—well, it's like stage fright. She won't even come in at night, wears jeans all the time—anything to avoid dealing with the public." He was so easy to talk to, it was hard to stop. Next she'd be reciting her grocery list.

"Which part of your job do you dislike most?" he asked.

"The hostessing, definitely. I hate running around in long gowns—"

"You look spectacular in them."

She felt a tremor of pleasure. "Thank you. And most of—"

"Of course, you look spectacular in those pants too."

"Thanks again," she said. The compliments felt wonderful. His nearness as they walked the hard-packed sand, the occasional brush of his fingers on her arm or shoulder when he gestured while talking, were making her breathe fast with anticipation, wanting more of his touch, much more.

What a roller-coaster of emotions in just two days! *It's as if I'm making up for lost time,* she thought. *Just yesterday I was grudgingly admitting to Barrie that maybe I should consider the idea of a relationship—and now here I am, praying this man will take me in his arms!*

"What were you saying about the gowns?" he prodded.

"Oh. Sorry," she said, starting guiltily, as if her thoughts had been on display. "I was saying that most of what I do is the usual hostess juggling act, and I do it well, but I've gotten so bored with it."

"I'd like to help you figure out what you'd prefer."

"I'd—like that," she answered, touched.

"That's partly a selfish offer," he said, slowing his pace, forcing her to slow hers.

"Why?" she asked, though she was quite sure she knew, and needles of joy were sending tingles all along her body.

"Because I want to help you past that problem so it

doesn't stand in the way of—us." He stopped and clasped her arms to halt her, turning her to face him. "Am I wrong, Lynn?" His eyes scanned her face in the near-blackness, looking for the answer there, for the confirmation of what his instinct told him. "Are you sending the message I think you are? Because I know what I'm receiving, and I feel that way too."

Courage sprouting from she knew not where, Lynn met his eyes and lifted her hands to his shoulders. He needed no further answer. With a deep moan of delight, he took her in his arms, and as his lips descended to meet hers, Lynn was filled with a sudden aching foreknowledge of how he would taste, his mouth heated but gentle, his tongue probing in intimate exploration, the tingle of salt from the constant cool spray mingling from her lips to his.

Imagination became reality as they stood together in the night mist, their mouths meeting, questing, knowing. *This is what all the agony is for,* Lynn thought wildly, dizzy with joy. For a long, long moment they kissed; finally Lynn broke gently away, overcome. She took a few unsteady steps toward the waterline and stood, shivering, bathed in pleasure, waiting for her racing heart to calm, her breathing to ease.

Soon she felt Reed behind her. She shuddered and then sighed with delight, wanting to melt into him. His hands came around her waist and she covered them with hers. He too seemed shaken, overwhelmed as she was by the power of their kiss, the emotions it had kindled. Pillowed in his strong warmth, secure, Lynn felt she could stay there all night.

Reed's mouth gently brushed against her forehead, then moved to the corner of her eye, along her cheek and the line of her chin. Teasingly he nibbled at the outer edge of her lips and then down, along her neck. Her head went back as his mouth burrowed under the edge of her blouse to find the nubbin of her collarbone and close on it. The softly insistent motion of his lips and tongue there caused tiny shocks of pleasure that made her gasp.

He raised his head, and his hands were tighter at her waist now, hugging her to him; she could feel the press of his own ardor at her back, and the excitement of her effect on him was galvanizing. She wanted to be fully in his arms again, to feel his body against her hips, her breasts. She moved out of his hold and turned to face him.

Now it was her lips that moved searchingly, wanting to taste, to express. Taking his face in her hands, she kissed the smooth skin beneath his chin, licked the beginning tickle of beard, tasted salt mixed with sharp maleness, then moved upward. Pulling his head lower, she buried her face in his heavy, silky hair, inhaling deeply, hungry for her fill of the smell that had tantalized her.

"Mmm," she purred near his ear.

He clasped her tighter. "Lynn," he whispered. "I wanted to hold you like this the moment I met you."

"I know," she said, and covered his lips with hers.

He answered with his tongue, softly forcing its way between her lips, tasting the satiny recesses of her mouth. When she met it with her own, he made a soft noise of longing and pressed the full length of her body to his, one hand on her back, the other across the slope of her derrière.

They explored each other's mouths with wonder and delight, the banquet of tastes and aromas causing Lynn to feel faint. Reed opened the belt of her coat and, as she stood vulnerable, her arms raised and her hands in his hair, eased her blouse out of her waist-band. Her breasts tingled, awaiting his touch. Lynn trembled between anxiety and pleasure, resisting the urge to lower her arms in self-protection; but his fingers sought the velvety heated skin of her waist and then moved downward, just a slight way beneath her waistband, to stroke the curving flare of her hips.

For several minutes he caressed her there, gently, and Lynn realized that this was a decision point. She shook her head weakly, trying to clear it. Her words to Barrie came back to her: *I don't know where it's headed, but I'm going to climb on and see what happens.* Well, she'd gotten on, all right—but she hadn't known it would be a super-express! Everything was happening so fast. There were so many sensations to be experienced; some her body had forgotten long ago, and others, she'd swear, she'd never known before. But then—why shouldn't it happen fast? That was how she felt. Frightened of this journey, but so anxious, so eager. If her emotions were hurtling at super-express speed, why shouldn't events match them?

It was all so mystifying. She rested her head against his shoulder.

"To be continued?" Reed whispered, closing her coat and retying the belt.

The breeze off the water was chilly on her damp face. *Yes, yes, yes,* her heart screamed, but her head urged caution. The tumult of this moment was no time to be handling such questions.

"I can't answer now," she said.

He kissed her nose. "Okay. Take all the time you need. Take ten minutes, twelve." His tone was bantering, but his eyes still glinted with yearning

He held her hand in his, and together they began to walk back toward the parking lot.

"Let's go back to my selfish offer," Reed said.

Selfish offer, her muddled brain echoed as she tried to orient herself.

"About helping you with your job dilemma."

Oh, that.

"Lynn?" He squeezed her hand in his big warm one. "Are you there?"

She drew in a chestful of the bracing briny air and let it out slowly.

"Maybe this will bring you back to life," he said. He stopped, clasped her shoulders, placed his lips softly on hers. One hand moved up to stroke her cheek.

After a moment she broke away. Her breathing was ragged, but no more so than his.

"Better?" he asked huskily.

"Worse," she whispered.

He took her hand and they started off again. The motion was calming and they walked quietly for several minutes, but Lynn knew from his tight, possessive grip that he was having as much trouble regaining his composure as she was.

Finally he said, "Maybe if we briskened the pace a little—"

She turned to him. "Briskened?"

"Isn't that a word?"

"Not unless you spell it differently and stew it with onions."

He chuckled. "Pretty quick for someone who couldn't have spelled her own name a couple of minutes ago."

"Me? Who's the one who suddenly can't speak English?"

He gave her a quick hug without breaking stride, and too soon they were back at the car. "Which hotel?" she asked as she started it.

"The Oceanside."

"Nice."

"Yeah. I wish I didn't have to check out in the morning."

She looked sharply at him. "You're checking out?"

"Didn't Barrie tell you?"

"No," she said, a mix of feelings descending.

"I have to go back to New York and tie up some loose ends. I didn't know at first whether it would be necessary, but I talked to my boss and he'd like me to. So I leave tomorrow, and I'll be back Thursday."

Relief flooded her. Thursday!

He leaned forward to peer at her face. "How long did you think I'd be gone?"

They'd reached his hotel and she pulled up in front. "I didn't know what to think."

"Let me give you something to think about," he said, taking her hand. In the pallid light of a street lamp she saw his eyes burn with feeling before he lowered his head and kissed the inside of her wrist, his lips leaving an invisible imprint that glowed with warmth. Then he looked up and said huskily, "You're an exquisite woman, Lynn, and one day very soon I'm going to kiss all of you that way."

She couldn't speak. She wanted only to hold him, to keep him there. The picture of his lips tasting all the secret parts of her that yearned for him made her feel faint.

He opened the door and climbed out. Ducking his head inside, he said, "Think about that while I'm in New York." The light shone on the tape that held his glasses together, and her heart turned over. He closed the door and was gone.

CHAPTER THREE

One more day, Lynn thought.

It was Wednesday night. The dining room had been cleaned and set for Thursday lunch. She ran a practiced eye over the tables, then went to check the reception room.

She'd replayed her beach walk with Reed a hundred times since Friday, reliving each stroke of his big hands on her fevered skin, his lips setting her face afire, the feel of his hard body as he held her urgently to him. Often she'd caught herself reddening or chuckling in her private reverie; Antal had cast her several knowing glances, Barrie wore a perpetual wink, and customers were beginning to look at her as if they were in some doubt of her sanity.

To Lynn, however, going from Miss Indifferent to someone who walked around in a constant state of desire was a little scary. Was it, as Barrie had said, just a matter of "the right guy coming along"?

Who knows? Lynn thought as she got into her car to drive home. All she cared about at the moment was the fact that it was Wednesday, which meant that tomorrow was Thursday, which was when Reed would be back.

She drove out to Route 1 and turned left, heading for Sycamore Street. Her apartment, an airy one-bedroom in an aging white-shingled house, was a comforting prospect; she always loved returning to its coziness, its cluttered-but-clean atmosphere that was so much a reflection of her. She could handle any crisis at work or deal with the most hostile customer, knowing her oasis waited. And now, with so many new things chipping away at her peace, its security was more important than ever.

She rolled down the car window. The tangy dampness of the night reminded her of—*Oh, everything reminds you of Reed.*

She turned into Sycamore, drove slowly along the night-quiet street. Somewhere an owl called. Except for the car's hum, it was the only sound in the hushed lateness. Already her tension was fading. She looked forward to reading more of the new mystery she'd bought yesterday.

She parked in the graveled area in back of the house, in her spot that never changed. There was a dark patch where her crankcase dripped slightly and the oil had accumulated over the years to form the familiar splotch that says, "This is where my car goes." She heard the owl again as she stepped out, taking her handbag and hostess outfit, and went upstairs to her apartment.

Turning the key, Lynn suddenly realized she was

standing in wetness. She looked down; water seeped from under the door. The entire landing was soaked.

She gasped and pushed the door open—and found a sodden mess. Dirty water covered her plush scatter rugs and the living room floor she kept polished to a winking gloss. Magazines and books, including the new mystery, floated forlornly. Running shorts she'd kicked off on her way to the shower that morning lay in a wet lump of reproof.

She threw down her handbag, hard. It landed with a loud and filthy splash that was so perversely satisfying, she hurled her hostess dress after it.

Her beautiful living room! Those lovely floors! So many of her things—dirty, soaked, ruined! She leaped on her dress, stamping on it, grinding it into the muck with her heel, thoroughly dousing herself.

Finally, exhausted and dripping, Lynn slumped against the doorframe. Now what? Now that she'd had her tantrum, spoiled a few more of her clothes, where did she start to straighten this mess out? She couldn't get the landlord; he was away. Besides, what would poor old Mr. Petrie do at this hour? The same thing she'd better do: find the problem and try to fix it.

With the silt for a clue, it didn't take Lynn long to discover that a bleeder valve had blown off the living room radiator. The heat had shut off hours ago, so there was no more water flowing out—but the furnace would send a fresh supply through the system when it went on in the morning. She couldn't get to it to turn it off with the landlord gone. She'd have to replace that valve.

Then she remembered. The tool shed! Mr. Petrie kept some spare radiator parts out there—she was sure she'd seen them.

Muttering about the slime, she pawed through the water for the damaged valve, located it, and went out to the shed. Awkwardly, balancing her flashlight, she got the combination padlock open on the second try.

Bless Mr. Petrie's neatness. If she'd had to sort through an anonymous jumble for a tiny part, she'd never have found it—but there on the wall, in a wooden holder of assorted hardware, was a valve that matched hers.

She went upstairs, threaded on the replacement, and surveyed the room once more. Her bedroom at least was dry; she could go to sleep, as her weary bones urged, and think about cleaning the apartment in the morning. The thought of falling into her soft bed and drifting off was so tempting; oblivion beckoned with seductive fingers. But no; she ought to mop now, get the excess water up so the wood wouldn't warp.

She washed the muddy splatters off her face and arms, put on old shorts and a T-shirt, and went to work barefoot with a sponge mop and bucket.

Call Reed, a voice whispered as she wiped and squeezed, wiped and squeezed. *He might have come back tonight.*

What for? she answered herself. *There's nothing he can do that I haven't already. Besides, I look like King Kong's sister.*

You didn't look much better sitting on a wet floor the first time he saw you, and he liked you then—he said so.

Admit it—this is the kind of rotten break that calls for a friendly face.

Yes, Mr. Graham had checked in, the groggy-sounding desk clerk informed her, and if she insisted, he'd ring the room, even though it *was* two in the morning. Was she aware of that?

"Are you aware that you're a rude and surly man?" she asked him, but he'd already made the connection and clicked off, and she found herself saying, "You're a rude and surly man" in Reed's ear.

There was a thunderclap of silence while Lynn mentally called herself names.

"Lynn? Is that you?"

"Yes. I'm sorry. You, um, weren't supposed to—when did you get in?" She swallowed. She hadn't been prepared for what his voice would do to her, the throaty rumble that, she remembered now, sounded even more intimate on the phone. A fluid heat washed over her, weakening her legs, and she had to sit down.

"About an hour ago. I came in tonight so I'd be rested for my solo debut tomorrow."

Of course, you nerd, the last thing he needs is to stay up mopping with you when he's starting a new job tomorrow.

"Right," she said, struggling to conjure up a reason for the call. "Well," she said, "I just, uh, wanted to remind you to bring . . . uh . . ."

"Bring what?"

"Your Social Security card," she finished desperately.

"I already gave the number to Barrie." He paused.

"Lynn, you don't call a new employee at two in the morning about a Social Security card."

"Is everybody going to keep pointing out to me that it's two in the morning?"

"What?"

"Never mind."

"You wanted to see me, didn't you? That's why you called."

Now she'd have to either tell the truth or look like a complete fool. "No, Reed," she said. "My apartment is flooded, and I called on the off-chance you'd gotten back to ask you to help me clean up. Then, when I saw how inconsiderate I was being—"

"You're really flooded? Give me directions. I'll be right there."

Her pulse jumped to four thousand, but she forced herself to demur. "Don't be silly, I can—"

"What's your address?"

"Fourteen Sycamore, but—"

"I'll get directions from the desk." He hung up.

"White wine or red?" Lynn asked him two hours later as they sprawled on the couch. She felt more tired than ever before, and heaven knew how Reed was going to stagger into the kitchen tomorrow—today!—but the room now looked habitable.

Reed had helped her wrestle the dripping rugs downstairs and hang them on the clothesline. Together they'd mopped, cleaned, salvaged what wasn't ruined.

"White," he answered.

"Second choice?"

"Red."

"Excellent." She pulled herself wearily up and poured two goblets of Burgundy.

"This would have taken me three times as long without you," she told him, sitting, her nervousness returning since she was no longer distracted by the work. She sipped her wine and saw the glass tremble. She set it on the side table, trying to keep her eyes away from the enticing picture he made, relaxing on the couch. Now that she knew how his body felt, could recall the contours of his pelvis and thighs as they pressed against her, she couldn't look at him leaning back like that without wanting to know those sensations again.

He reached over and ran his fingertips up and down the side of her neck. "Is that really the only reason you called?"

She didn't answer, couldn't. Her breathing quickened.

He took off his still-taped glasses, set them aside, and leaned closer, his eyes inches from hers. "Is it?" His mouth replaced his fingers and he gently nipped the smooth flesh of her neck, pushing her curls aside. Her head went back, almost of its own accord. "Answer me," he demanded harshly in her ear.

"No," she managed.

He nibbled the line of her jaw, found her mouth, kissed it gently, sweetly. With a long sigh that was almost a groan, Lynn wrapped her arms around his neck and their tongues met, darting, tasting. Lynn suddenly knew a hunger unlike any she'd ever felt for food, and she didn't want to let him go, wouldn't release his lips and tongue to explore elsewhere. For long minutes she spun in a vortex of pleasure. Her fingers, newly supersensitive, became aware of a trembling deep within the sinews of Reed's muscled arms, the simmer of barely banked passion.

His big hands went under her T-shirt, caressing, barely touching; she could almost feel her skin expand as if reaching out for more. With a firm and easy motion he unhooked her bra and she arched toward him expectantly, eager for his touch on her breasts. But instead he stroked her back, pressing her nearer.

"I want to hear you say why you called me," he whispered.

She drew back so she could see his face. Every muscle felt heated, liquid, and she could barely focus. She gave up and reached to clasp him to her again, but he grasped her upper arms and held her away.

"Say it," he told her quietly.

"I . . . wanted to see you."

He shook his head impatiently, and waited.

She could no more have held back now than she could have turned invisible. Every last nugget of reluctance had floated away.

"I wanted you," she told him boldly at last, her eyes never wavering from his. "I wanted to make love with you, feel your hands on me. I wanted—"

But he could no longer hold himself apart from her, this man whose face had just shown her what kind of pleasure her heartfelt words had ignited. He pushed her back against the couch with a moan that signaled a hunger to match her own and crushed his lips down onto hers, seeking her tongue, seeming to want to devour her. His hands went back under her shirt, eagerly reaching, to answer her craving, and found her breasts.

She moved against his touch like a cat, arching, stretching, some ancient instinct guiding her to fit herself to his hands. She was on fire now, totally his.

He pulled her shirt over her head and she twisted to help him, shrugging out of her bra. Now she knelt on the couch, naked but for her shorts. They'd opened the windows to freshen the apartment, and the cold night air, combined with all the sensations Reed's hands had aroused, made her breasts feel exquisitely tender. She had a momentary urge to cover herself, change her position to one that felt less vulnerable, but she ignored it. Reed leaned over and held her waist with both hands, frankly gazing; the admiration she saw in his face caused a flicker of embarrassment and then a wash of happiness.

"You're magnificent," he said, and she could see his chest move as his breath came rapidly. He bent and nipped at her breast, his lips moving with a deliberate gentleness, as if he was trying to stay in control, keep his desire leashed until he chose to free it. He took each breast in his mouth, caressing with his lips and tongue, scraping softly with his teeth, until she thought she might collapse. Seeming to sense the weakness that was stealing over her, Reed eased her back against the couch.

She reached for him, wanting to feel his weight on her, but he drew away.

"I made a promise to you that I'd like to keep now," he said, running a teasing finger around the inside of her waistband.

Lynn couldn't seem to get her breathing back to a rate that would let her talk. She reached for him again. All she wanted was to feel his body stretched out over hers, the hard planes of his limbs imprinting themselves on her flesh . . .

He evaded her arms. The hand that had been making inroads at her waist was now stroking the very top of her thigh under her shorts, causing a fire to burn deep inside her.

"Do you remember what I said the other night?" he asked. "In your car?"

His hand was inching closer to her center now, that place where all her longing had suddenly seemed to pool, and she shifted her body to meet it, but again he was maddeningly elusive.

"I said I was going to kiss all of you," he told her, and bent his head. He eased her shorts just past her navel and trailed a warm line of kisses along her midriff. Down again came the shorts, just another infuriating inch, and he licked her hip bones as her sweet torment grew.

When his palm pressed her belly she cried out with pleasure, and an instant later he was pulling her shorts off all the way and she was arching, writhing. Then his mouth and hands were where she had longed to have them, and rivers of fire were coursing through her, setting her body aflame. She shut her eyes and gave herself over to his tongue, his fingers, the mad joy of his loving.

Suddenly she knew she had to stop him now, pull back, ease herself down if they were to join and share, and she tried to push him away, struggling for the words to say what her body was shouting. But he ignored her feeble efforts and his motions became even more insistent, contradicting her message, telling her they had oceans of time for sharing, that this was her moment and all the sharing he wanted was in this loving gift.

Abandoning herself completely to the liquid shivers radiating from her core, she cried out again, more loudly this time, her hands tangling in his hair, her legs trembling. Her entire body felt streaked with heat as waves of almost unendurable delight washed over her again and again and she thrashed about, delirious with pleasure.

As her shudders slowly ebbed, Reed's movements grew more gentle, tender again, in perfect concert with her sensations. She remembered her thoughts as they'd begun their beach walk, how he'd matched his stride to hers, and she laughed softly. Was that just a few days ago? If she'd had any inkling then that that ability could have such intimate significance . . .

"Was that a chuckle?" Reed asked.

"Yes," she said, but was suddenly too shy to tell him what had made her laugh, this man with whom she'd just enjoyed the deepest closeness possible.

"Well," he said, "stay happy, because I haven't finished yet—with this." He took her hand and kissed her wrist as he had in the car. "I still have a lot of beautiful territory to cover."

His lips began to move up the inside of her forearm and she snuggled down into the cushions of the couch, almost purring with contentment, feeling cuddly and affectionate. But by the time his mouth had blazed its way all the way up, to tenderly bite her shoulder and explore the silky dampness underneath, darts of flame were once more invading her body.

"You're delicious," he said huskily in her ear. "I can't look at you without wanting to do this." He kissed his way down her other arm, his tongue tracing circles on the velvety surface, and when he reached her hand he took each finger in his mouth.

Lynn's desire was reaching a fever pitch again, and she felt urges of her own. This time, when she reached for him and he tried to resist, she was insistent. She pushed away his questing hands and began working on his shirt buttons. The fact that she was totally naked while he was still dressed had its appeal—the sensation of his rough clothing on her skin was a shivery surprise—but she wanted his flesh now, as he had enjoyed hers.

She took off his shirt. The expanse of smooth skin, with its covering of reddish-brown hair, was devastating, and she pushed him back, eager to taste. He lay there while she covered the muscular hardness with kisses, his breath quickening. His hands stroked her hair, her neck, her back, and she felt the same tremor within him as she had earlier. When her kisses reached his waist and she moved to unbuckle his belt, he groaned and eased her away, then stood, pulling her upright.

He took her hand and led her to the bedroom. She hesitated in the doorway. "Should we turn the light out?" she asked.

"Yes," he said, bending to move her hair aside and kiss the back of her neck. "I want to use all my senses with you, to smell and taste and feel. I want to know you in the dark and have you know me."

Together they reached the bed and lay down, moving as one person. Now, finally, she could glory in the feel of his body aligned full length with hers, his bigness, his power, enveloping her. She pulled herself close, straining to fit against him head to toe. He rolled onto his back and took her with him, holding her so she lay on top of him, his hands exploring her back, her derrière, her thighs. Then he rolled them back again so his body covered hers, and she gasped, the pleasure of his weight, his aroma that was so unmistakable, the insistent pressure of his desire filling her with passion.

Just a short while ago she'd reached the peak of delight, scaled the heights in a way she never had—and now here she was again, as if there had been no satisfaction at all, yearning for more of Reed, breathlessly anticipating even greater joy. Oh, these feelings weren't foreign, she'd had pleasurable experiences in the past—but not like this, never anything approaching the unalloyed happiness she'd known already with this unbearably sensual man.

She wanted all of him now, wanted to know his

body as he knew hers. She was pushing at him, trying to find her voice so she could tell him to finish undressing. Finally he seemed to remember that he still wore his pants. He stood and removed them, and then his shorts. For a moment she wished the room weren't dark, but then he was beside her again and nothing mattered but the warmth of his skin, the firmness of his rough, muscular legs against her smooth ones, the intimacy of his maleness.

She sensed his hesitation, that he was trying hard to restrain himself, but she was more than ready, as eager as he. She'd known the ultimate pleasure, but the supreme sweetness of sharing his pleasure still waited.

Silently she moved her body against him in a way that told him what he wanted to know. He understood immediately and poised himself above her, his breathing heavy, her own halted as she waited in precious agony for him to take her.

"Lynn," he said, and slid his hands underneath to lift her to meet his first thrust. She could feel his mammoth effort to hold back, to spare her the full force of his passion so as not to hurt her, but his emotions were too much for him and, expelling his breath in a rush, he plunged ahead.

Lynn felt an instant of fear at his unleashed strength, but immediately it was replaced by a rapture more enthralling than anything she'd ever known. Reed's maleness filled her, electrified her. She was stunned by the beauty of his need for her, the glorious power of this act of possession.

Her own body was once again crying out for release,

moving faster against him, rising to meet him. The tumultuous spasms began, peaking higher and higher, and Lynn felt herself spiraling toward a crest that was hers and Reed's, the essence of ecstasy for the two of them alone.

"Lynn," he said again, and this time her name was a rush of breath in her ear, raspy with the blade of passion, as she felt him answer her tremors with the start of his own explosive release. She gripped him with her legs and arms, and their cries mingled as they knew the wonder of their destination together.

The dawn sounds filtered through the open windows and surrounded them as they lay on her bed: the soft rustling of insects, the new-day cries of birds. Reed shifted himself and Lynn so that they lay belly-down with their arms around each other, and as she floated into sleep, she heard him whisper her name a final time.

CHAPTER FOUR

Lynn pulled into the Gull House drive. The car window was open and she sang along with the radio, loudly enough to startle some sparrows pecking on the grass. They flapped off in a huff, and she smiled as she parked. The old Lynn wouldn't have been singing loudly enough to wake an ant.

So much had happened in this brief time, she still couldn't absorb it all. Something told her not to try. The more she analyzed what she was doing, her crazy new reactions, the way a current zinged through her every time she saw Reed or thought of him . . . the more likely she'd be to back off. And after Wednesday, that magic night . . . she wanted only more of the same. Barrie always complained that she had to be dragged into new things, her heels leaving furrows in the dirt. Well, no one was dragging her now. She was ready for love this time, *ready* . . .

"Ready!" she shouted, and hopped out of the car.

"What?"

"Barrie? I didn't see you," Lynn said, embarrassed. The burgeoning June foliage was starting to climb the sides of the little porch, and she'd been hidden. "What are you doing here so close to dinner?"

"Leaving. I just stopped to sniff, the air smelled so good. What are you smiling at?"

"Was I smiling?"

"You still are."

"Oh. I was thinking of a joke."

"What joke?"

Lynn looked off toward the trees. "The one about the, ah, kangaroo and the . . ."

"You're making this up. And you're still smiling."

Lynn made a fierce face and they both laughed.

"It's nice to see you in such a good mood all the time." Barrie peered at Lynn, as if the reason could be found etched somewhere in her face. "Not that any two-year-old couldn't guess why."

She glanced nervously toward the kitchen. "Keep your voice down."

"He's not in there."

"Where'd he go?" Lynn asked, ostentatiously casual.

"To pick up something for one of the specials. And you do a terrible I-couldn't-care-less." Barrie got into her car. "He'll be back, I promise. Nobody kidnapped him. See you tomorrow."

Lynn went through the kitchen and up to her dressing room. She changed into a hostess dress the color of the Caribbean and stroked on the precisely matched eye shadow she'd just searched three stores for. Then plenty of mascara . . . now that she had someone to bat her eyelashes for, she needed something to bat.

She fluffed her glossy dark curls with a brush. *You never used to spend this much time on your looks in a week,* she chided herself. *You act like you're getting ready for the Academy Awards. Every night.*

Her long legs moving beneath the swirl of peacock challis, she went quickly down the stairs. She looked over the dining room, propped up some carnations, straightened a few settings. In the reception area she checked the reservations book—just about full, good for a June Saturday. As long as there weren't too many walk-ins, dinner would go well.

A couple of the waitresses were muttering behind her. "Scrod with *who?*" she heard one say. "At Gull House?" another exclaimed.

She turned. They were reading a blackboard propped on an easel in the corner of the room, next to the dining room entrance.

In neatly chalked block letters it said:

*** SPECIALS ***
MONKFISH POACHED IN SWEET VERMOUTH
SHRIMP SAUTEED WITH RED PEPPERS AND CAPERS
SCROD WITH PEANUTS, THAI STYLE
MUSSELS AND LITTLENECKS IN GREEN SAUCE

Surprised anger welled in her throat. Where had he —oh, it was the kitchen blackboard, the one they used to note what had to be ordered. He'd spiffed it up and cleaned the food spatters off the easel. But the nerve! Roger would never have offered such unusual dishes without asking her, and the specials were always recited by the waitresses, not scribbled on a blackboard. What did he think this was, the Left Bank?

She stalked to the kitchen and pushed open the door. Reed looked up from his chopping block, and the blaze of his green eyes was like a beacon, weakening her. He grinned.

"My first-night solo. Come to wish me luck?"

His presence was overwhelming, entrancing, and she ground her teeth in vexation. He wasn't wearing his apron. Comfortable-looking black slacks fit as if he'd been dropped into them, and the sleeves of his plaid shirt were rolled up, leaving bare an enticing patch of hairy forearm.

"I wanted to talk to you about the blackboard," Lynn said.

His grin widened. "Nice, huh? All I did was scrub it up a little, and it looks like new. We could get a cheap one for in here, or maybe—"

"I don't want a blackboard out there. We don't announce our specials that way. And that's the other thing. I wish you'd asked me before you decided on them. They're not what our people are used to at all."

His smile was gone and his face was set in determined lines. He put down his knife. "Are we going to go through this again?"

Lynn sighed. "You say that as though I'm a faulty dashboard light that won't stay fixed. I'm the one with the reason to be mad." Her voice was rising along with her anger. She made herself shut up. She'd be damned if she'd entertain the staff yet again. "Let's go out back."

"You got it." He preceded her out the door, his shoes hitting the linoleum with unnecessary force.

The soft air calmed Lynn a little. She followed Reed across the pebbled lot to a stand of lilac bushes. Their perfume enveloped her, the sweetness clinging like a silken garment.

"You still seem to have your own ideas about what to cook," she told him, "when I've made it clear again and again that—"

"Of course I have my own ideas about what to cook! What chef—"

She waved a hand impatiently. His dazzle was muddling her so that she couldn't even say what she meant. "Wait. I'm not putting this the right way. It's innovations I'm talking about. They aren't welcome, and you can't say you didn't know that."

"I didn't! Not in terms of—"

"What? How many times have we been over—"

"Lynn, hold it," he said more quietly. He took off his glasses, realized he was holding them by the fragile mended earpiece, and quickly switched. "I don't want to fight with you." Heat surged between them. Even through her anger, Lynn ached for the contact their bodies demanded. But he seemed to know that wasn't the way to settle this, and he kept his hands busy with his glasses.

"I don't want to fight either, but—"

"Damn it, *wait.*" Now he did touch her, a big hand firmly holding her shoulder. Though it was meant to restrain, Lynn felt every nerve erupt with longing. "We're talking about two different things," he said. "I know you don't want me fooling around with regular menu items. I won't say I agree with that, but I—"

"Where do you get off—"

"Are you going to let me talk?" he asked tightly, gripping her shoulder harder. "You said you didn't want to argue, but so far I only count one person keeping his temper. If this is your idea of how not to fight, I hope nobody ever appoints you to the diplomatic corps."

Lynn stepped back, out of reach of that maddening hand. She didn't know which she was reacting to more, his presumptuousness or his galvanic touch; but one or the other or both were sending shocks through her system, frazzling her. It was hard to pull herself together and join his effort to be reasonable.

He studied her face. What he saw there must have convinced him she was ready to listen. "As I was saying," he went on, "I know you didn't want me changing the status quo, but I didn't realize I had to kneel and pray to it. How could I know I wasn't supposed to make any innovations at all? Who would hire a good chef and then tie his hands to his ankles? Serving new things when people are expecting the usual is one thing, but why can't they be offered as choices?"

Lynn tried to match his rational tone. "I realize you're frustrated, but I just can't see changing something that works. This is a traditional operation. People who want canary livers a la Grecque can pick from half a dozen nouvelle places, but everyone knows Gull House is *the* choice for classic seafood. The volume of our business proves that."

"Business is good, but it could be even better. There are so many exciting things we could do. If you'd only see—"

He turned away. Tension showed in the knotted sinews of his back and shoulders through the shirt, and her head told her he was trying to quell his temper. But her body perceived him in a different way. On the sensuous plane of imagination she removed his shirt and laid her cheek against his fragrant flesh. She massaged away the tightness in the large muscles, her fingers alternately kneading and stroking. As she felt him begin to relax, her mouth replaced her hands. Slowly she felt another sort of tension build under the velvety skin, the tautness of desire. As he turned back to her, she saw it in his face, the simmering heat that had brought her to such heights on that wonderful night.

But now he was really turning to face her, the real Reed in the parking lot, and regretfully Lynn let the fantasy Reed slide away.

He said, "Let's drop this. We're not going to make any sense to each other angry."

"Okay," Lynn said, and reluctantly started back. There was so much to do; she was way behind. But it was agony to tear herself away from Reed, even when they were mad.

"Wait," he said. She thought that must be the sweetest word in the language. "I'd like to—what are you doing Monday?"

It was the first day of their "weekend"; the restaurant was closed Monday and Tuesday.

"Nothing," she said.

"I'd like to bury the hatchet by cooking just for you. How about a picnic?"

"A picnic," she repeated foggily, as if he'd said "a jailbreak." Then her mind clicked back in. "A picnic! That sounds wonderful." She smiled at him. "Terrific idea. I'd love to!"

"Sorry to see you're so ambivalent," he said, and she whacked his arm. "I'll pick you up at one. Shouldn't be any problem finding your place again—especially in daylight." Their gazes met for an incandescent few seconds while her memory—and his, she knew by the flush on his cheeks—returned to that enchanted night in her apartment. Then, without speaking, she went back inside and to work.

How much cooking can he do in a place he just moved into two days ago? Lynn wondered, rubbing her hair with a towel.

Aromatic clouds of steam swirled around her in the bathroom, and she raised the misted window. There was Mr. Petrie weeding his impatiens beds . . . and there, for heaven's sake, was Reed, in the used green Dodge he'd bought, just pulling into the driveway.

She raced into the bedroom, yanked on the striped pullover she'd laid out, and tried to get quickly into her jeans. But they were newly washed and snug, and with her skin still damp, Lynn was hopping around the room in her effort to pull them all the way up. In the middle of her dance she realized she'd forgotten her underpants. She pulled off the jeans, put on the pants, tried again. *No, you aren't nervous or anything,* she raged at herself. *The kindergarten task of putting on your clothes is just a little beyond you, that's all.*

The doorbell rang. "Just a second," she called. She made herself count to ten, then zipped her pants at last. She glanced into the mirror. Dark wet straggles framed a naked pale face. She sighed.

"Sorry I'm early," Reed said when she opened the door. "Got my errands done faster than I expected, and I didn't think you'd mind—since we know each other so well." He was having a good long look as he spoke, surveying her lissome legs in the tight jeans, her bare feet, and the band of ivory midriff where her pull-over had ridden up as she wrestled with the pants.

Finally his eyes moved high enough to notice her hair. "Just out of the shower?" he asked, grinning.

"No, this is the wet look."

He nodded, taking her seriously.

"Have a seat while I stick the safety pin through my nose."

She closed the door and went to the bedroom. He followed. Catching on, he said, "I guess that means you're a little irked that I'm here already."

"What, me irked?" She began to towel her hair again. She smiled; she couldn't help it. He made her happy. "I just wanted to look nice when you got here."

"You don't think you look nice now?"

"With no face? I look like I died last week."

He chuckled and took the towel from her. "Let me do that."

Before she could say anything, he was toweling for

her, a section at a time, rather than rubbing her head. "The less you have on, the better you look. Those bare feet knocked me out when you opened the door. I guess because of—last week. It reminded me."

Her face burned. With him here in her bedroom, moving around it familiarly, that was all she could think of too. *If he touches my skin, it will singe his hand,* she thought.

He lifted her hair from her neck and softly kissed her there. Her knees nearly buckled. She grabbed the dresser for support and caught a glimpse of them in the mirror, his body curved over hers as he nuzzled her nape. She turned to face him and his arms went around her. When their lips met, Lynn was flooded with a honeyed tide, a rush of such delight that she would have crumpled to the floor if Reed hadn't been holding her so tightly.

He broke away, took a handful of her moist hair, and pressed it to his face. "You smell wonderful," he whispered. "And if I don't knock this off, you'll never get me out of here."

She started to tell him that wouldn't be a bad idea at all, but he added, "I've been looking forward to showing off my cooking for you," and she stayed silent. She was still trembling a little. He went back to toweling her hair, his fingers feeling for the damp parts and pushing and fluffing the drier areas into place.

She let him do it. The confident way his hands moved over her head was nearly as sensuous as his kiss had been.

Finally he was done. He leaned against the wall and

folded his arms, content to watch while she did her makeup and finished dressing, but she shooed him out. Some privacy was a must. She needed time for her breathing to quiet and her quaking hands to still. If she tried to do her face in this condition, she'd have mascara in her nostrils.

They left the apartment and went downstairs. Mr. Petrie looked up from his masses of pink and white blooms and smiled, and Lynn introduced the tanned, wiry old man to Reed. The smile widened until he beamed. Lynn thought, *Can the whole world tell I'm having an affair? Is there some neon signal everyone can see?*

"Where are we going?" she asked as they climbed into the Dodge. She noticed a huge cooler in the backseat.

"The Marginal Way, I thought."

"What a great idea. I haven't been there in ages."

Reed turned onto Route 1 and headed north into Ogunquit Center. Even though it wasn't high season yet, vacationers thronged the little village. He turned right, toward the shore, and they parked in a municipal lot. He took a blanket from the trunk and they started along the historic walkway, the cooler between them.

The paved path snaked through the bluffs high above the ocean. A hundred feet down the craggy outcroppings, the surf slammed and sprayed, and they paused at every spot between the rocks and dunes where the view was good. Each vantage point was more splendid than the last. Reed seemed to know when Lynn was going to stop even before it happened, so there was no awkwardness with the heavy hamper. Her mind harked back to the first time she'd noted his knack for anticipating her rhythm . . . and the second.

"This looks just right," Reed said, pulling her from her memories. They'd come to a grassy spot nestled among some short dunes, screened from the public path but with a perfect view of the Atlantic.

They spread the blanket and sat. Bright sun winked off the water; the air was alive with tastes of spring and the tang of the sea. Lynn hadn't bothered to blow-dry her hair after Reed's toweling, and dampish strands brushed her cheeks in the breeze.

Her eyes kept moving from the view to Reed to the cooler. There were so many treats piquing her senses at once.

"Hungry?" he asked, starting to unpack. "I sure am. I've been working on this stuff all morning and trying not to sample too often."

"I'm impressed that you put your kitchen in shape so fast. If I'd moved into an apartment two days ago, any guest of mine would be lucky to get a cheese sandwich."

He shrugged, grinned. "That's my turf. It's what I fix up first. I still have cartons stacked in the bedroom and socks all over the couch, but I could put out a state dinner in that kitchen."

"Is it big?"

"Tiny. Not enough room to swing a trout. But it's nice; comfortable to work in. You'll have to see it."

"I'd like to."

His eyes caught hers as they both continued that thought along its natural path. Lynn felt that warm tremor starting again. She lowered her eyes to break the spell. Exactly the wrong move: there were his thighs, prominently displayed in denim as he knelt by the hamper. She looked back up, not too far, unwilling to meet his eyes again, only to see mounded biceps that stretched his shirt sleeves. She gave up and stared in fascination at him while he unpacked.

"—wouldn't have been right," she heard him say. He put a soup bowl in front of her.

She rolled her mental tape back, trying to catch the rest. No luck. She hadn't heard a word on any level.

"I'm sorry. Say that again?"

"Where were you?"

Coasting down your biceps. "Woolgathering," she said.

"Oh. Well, gather some of this." He spooned pale green liquid into her bowl from a container packed in ice. A nutlike aroma reached her. "Cream of avocado soup. I was saying that the china is a pain to carry, but for this feast paper and plastic wouldn't have been right."

"He said modestly. What's in these other containers?"

"Bay scallop salad, cheese biscuits, and strawberries in honey and Cointreau. And this," he said, taking out a covered pitcher, "margaritas." He poured one for her and floated a lime slice on top.

She sipped her drink and tasted the chilled soup. It was heaven. He produced a small pepper mill.

"Am I overdoing it?" he asked.

She laughed and shook her head. He ground pepper into her soup and they ate in quiet.

Gulls dived, squalling. One settled on a rock twenty feet down; they watched it use its legs as landing gear.

"Did you see that wing action?" Reed said. "Eight separate motions to fold them."

"I didn't see. Really?"

"It happens so fast you have to look closely. They get folded back in layers. Here's another one—watch."

The bird landed near the first, and Lynn saw the rapid feathering as it settled its wings. "Incredible," she said.

He handed her a plate. Whole cuplike leaves of red-tipped lettuce held the scallop salad. The white morsels were interspersed with dices of pimiento and red onion, and everything glistened with vinaigrette. It was delicious, the dressing sharp and mustardy.

"Biscuit?" Reed passed her the napkin-lined box of flaky golden rounds.

"I still don't see how you made all these things in a kitchen that doesn't know you yet," Lynn said. "Everything is wonderful. This is the best lunch I've ever had."

His smile stretched across his face. "And you haven't even had dessert."

She started to josh him back, then restrained herself. *This is the one guy in ten thousand who, when he says dessert, means strawberries,* she thought.

After lunch they stretched out on the blanket. Reed bunched his light jacket into a pillow for Lynn. The afternoon sun was warm despite the peppy breeze off the water, and a while later she sat up to remove her sneakers and socks. When she lay back down her shirt rode up, and before she could rearrange it Reed kissed the velvet skin above her navel. She closed her eyes and enjoyed the fuzzy pleasure of his tongue tracing a moist course along her waist.

She'd grown drowsy from the margaritas and the sun. She stretched under his touch, totally relaxed. Radiant tingles were beginning to inflame her skin where his lips and hands were busy. She'd never felt so good. Why had she waited so long to risk a real relationship, to chance giving her feelings free rein? How much glory had she missed all these years?

"Everything's perfect," she murmured sleepily.

"Hmm?" He pulled her shirt back into place and lay full-length beside her.

"This day. It's so lovely. The weather, the food—"

"The company?"

"Of course the company."

"You don't like me," he asked softly in her ear, "just because I'm hot stuff in the kitchen?"

She chuckled, enjoying having him so close.

"That was a great lunch, though." He rolled onto his back. "Seafood salads with vinaigrette—you can do so much more with those than with the mayonnaise type. We should put one on the menu—at least for lunch, just for starters. The avocado soup too. Or if you don't want to go that far out, I could try an oyster bisque with—"

"What are you doing?" Lynn sat abruptly upright.

He raised his head and shrugged. "Just thinking out loud, I guess. What's the matter?"

Lynn felt the faint chill of betrayal in her belly. She swallowed hard.

"Hey. You okay?"

"I'm not sure."

Immediately he sat up too. "Is your stomach upset?"

"You could say that," she allowed with a wry smile. She was fighting to control the rush of anger that threatened. Was it her imagination, was she being paranoid—or was he trying to take advantage in a big way?

"You look so uncomfortable," Reed said, his brow furrowed. "Maybe you should lie down."

"Lying down wouldn't help the kind of uncomfortable I feel."

"Well, what is it? Tell me."

She rubbed her forehead, as if to force herself to think clearly by erasing the murk inside. "What you said about putting a new salad and soup on the menu . . ."

"Yes?"

"That's what's bothering me."

He shook his head. "I don't understand," he said, but his face told her he was beginning to, and she felt her temper building defensively.

"You said you wanted to have a picnic so you could

cook just for me." She was trying to keep her voice down, but she saw his eyes harden, and the last of her control trickled away. "Cook just for me! Sure! Me today—half the population of Maine next week! If I'd known this was going to be a presentation, I'd have come prepared to take notes!"

"Lynn, for crying out loud, I didn't mean—"

"You didn't mean for me to catch on." She reached for a sock and jammed her foot into it. Her hands shook.

Now his face was darkening. "What are you so upset about? Do you actually think I invited you out just to be political? What kind of a crud do you think I am?"

"The kind of crud who has more ambition than brains." She struggled madly with her sneaker lace, wishing she could yank it out and use it around his neck.

He jumped up. "That's a lousy thing to say! Can't I mention anything about Gull House without you reacting as though I want to turn it into a video arcade?"

Now she was on her feet too. "What you want to turn it into is bad enough! Barrie and I didn't break our backs making it what it is to have you come along and gimmick it up like every other tourist trap. And I *don't* like being manipulated!"

"Will you just—"

"Will you just jump off a cliff? What good luck, we're on one. Thanks again," she yelled bitingly, "for the nice lunch you planned just for me!" She took off along the winding path, back the way they'd come, her rubber soles slapping the blacktop. Hurt and rage boiled in her chest. She sprinted until she was winded, then slowed to a jog, glancing back to see whether he'd followed. Not that she wanted him to—you'd just think the man might care to make sure she didn't twist an ankle or anything. By the time she'd covered the mile and a half to her house, there was still no sign of him. Fortunately. Who needed more of his pushiness?

Mr. Petrie had gone in. Good thing. She couldn't have managed even a fake smile. Muttering to herself, she opened her apartment door and flopped on the couch, still breathless from the run. *Oh, Reed, you jerk!*

CHAPTER FIVE

Lynn picked morosely at her dish of tuna straight from the can. *Cat food,* she thought. *You live like a cat. No one can get near you except on your terms. Your security comes before everything.*

She dumped the tuna in the trash.

She'd moped around the apartment for an hour after running home. She found things to do, dumb jobs that busied her hands. Finally, after painstakingly mending a pillowcase that should have been thrown out—it was worn so thin she could have watched television through it—she'd admitted what she was really doing: waiting to hear from Reed. She'd known then that she had to get out of the house. More than her hands needed to be occupied. She was mad, sad, upset—and looking for Reed to make a move so that she wouldn't have to decide what *she* wanted.

So she'd taken the car and run errands. It was nothing more stimulating than the make-work she'd done at home, but at least this was more distracting. In the Route 1 beach traffic, she'd actually stopped thinking about Reed for three or four minutes.

Then she'd come home and made dinner, such as it

was, and the few bites she'd managed had gone down like Styrofoam.

Now it was nearly dark, and the night bugs were beginning their chorus. She went into the bedroom and pushed the window higher. Through the screen floated fresh earth and plant odors, the ting of salt. *Reed.* The spring evening smells, the sounds of the live things, were too much. His presence was so strong. She glanced at the mirror over her dresser and saw his ghost leaning there, against the wall next to it, after he'd dried her hair. She raised a hand to her hair, stroked it as he had, and felt the threatening sting of tears.

"You're the jerk," she told the mirror, her voice loud in the hush that never used to seem empty to her. She leaned closer to the glass. Her face was paler, set in different lines from the morning. Defensive lines.

She rushed to the door and pulled it open. The draft from the landing window was chilly, and she ran back in for a jacket. She threw it over her shoulders, not stopping to put her arms in, and hurried down the stairs.

She started the car, and noticed her hands were shaking yet again. This was the third time today. First with desire, then anger, now—what? Regret. Anticipation. Maybe anger again—at herself. It had taken her so long to feel these powerful things for a man. The last two weeks had been the most exciting of her life. Yet her impulse to stay secure, repel the invasion, was still so strong, she'd almost let it put her right back where she'd been before. No fury, no hurt—but no love either. Certainly not the joyous heights, the sheer rapture she'd begun to know . . . and that she'd be a fool to toss away.

She backed to the end of the driveway and paused to let a car pass in the street. His apartment was on Ridge Place. She was pretty sure she knew where that was, down off the winding road that led to 1A.

She realized the car wasn't passing. It had stopped, and the driver seemed to be waiting.

Then in a flash of recognition she saw the Dodge's silhouette in the street light and Reed's face as he lowered the window. Her heart soared. She threw the Chevette into Park, jumped out, and ran to him.

"I thought I blew it," he said. His strong arms were around her, almost crushing her. She pressed herself even harder against him, her limbs turned to jelly with happy relief. It hadn't been too late! He'd missed her too! He couldn't bear for them to be apart any more than she could!

They stood, bonded, neither willing to let go. There were a hundred things Lynn wanted to say.

She heard the tick of the screen door opening and raised her head from Reed's chest. Mr. Petrie stood in the porch light's beam, his face a study in polite confusion. Two cars with their engines running, one half out of the driveway, the other in the middle of the street, humming noisily in the quiet night. Two people in the yard, gripping each other as though they were on the deck of the *Titanic*.

Lynn broke away.

Mr. Petrie seemed to be mentally sorting through

appropriate questions. "Is everything all right?" he asked finally.

"Fine," Lynn said, striving for a confident note, to reassure him there was no cause for worry. And then, because he looked disappointed that he wasn't going to learn anything more about this perplexing tableau, she added, "I was leaving to visit Reed, and what a coincidence! He was just coming here." She realized that hardly explained the abandoned cars gulping gas, or their passionate public embrace. She started to explain that they hadn't seen each other in a while, remembered she'd introduced him to Reed that morning, and stopped.

Reed rescued her. "We're just real glad to be together," he said with a big grin, and Mr. Petrie grinned back, dipped his head, and went inside.

They parked the cars and went upstairs, hand in hand.

"You didn't really think this was all an act to get my way at Gull House, did you?" Reed asked as soon as they were in Lynn's apartment.

"No," she said.

"I couldn't believe you'd ever think I was that sleazy."

"I didn't. It just came out that way because I was so mad."

He pulled off his glasses and started to reach for her. But he'd used the mended earpiece, and now it dangled, broken again.

"Let me try to fix that," Lynn said, seeing his frustration and wanting to help, even though the thought of his arms was alluring.

"Me Tarzan," he said, following her into the bedroom. "I'm supposed to be the mechanical one. You don't have to do this."

"Shut up and go bake some bread," she said. She picked layers of tape from the glasses' tiny hinge and rubbed off the leftover goo. She fitted the two pieces together. "It just needs something to go through . . . wait." She took out her sewing box and rummaged among cloth scraps and thread spools for a small safety pin.

She pushed it through the hinge and snapped it closed. "See?" she said triumphantly, moving the earpiece back and forth. "Now you can even fold them. What would you do without me?"

"I don't know," he said with such bare emotion that they just stared at each other for a long minute.

He put the glasses on. "I just know I never felt so miserable from one crummy fight in my life. You thought I was pushing you. I'm sorry."

"I did feel pushed, but I shouldn't have reacted like such a bobcat. I felt attacked." She went to the window and leaned on the sill. The evening breeze was refreshing on her face.

"Look," she said into the screen, "I know I'm too rigid. I'm trying not to be."

He waited.

"Do you want to call a press conference? Because I think I'm going to compromise."

She heard him chuckle behind her. "I wouldn't touch that with a flagpole."

She turned to him. "I don't want to change the menu." His disappointment showed. "This is only going to be a compromise, not a miracle. I thought maybe we could go with the blackboard business after all. A few specials a night, whatever you want to make." He smiled again and she returned it. "Then maybe you won't be so frustrated, and I can stop feeling like the wicked witch of the Northeast."

"Sounds good." He caressed her cheek with the backs of his fingers. "That wasn't so awful, was it?"

"No." She wanted him closer.

"Maybe you and I could sort of make a habit of that."

"Of what?" She'd agree to anything. Wearing snowshoes. Breeding minks.

"Compromising. Instead of overreacting and yelling and running from each other. Because I care so much, Lynn, and I don't want us to be making each other crazy."

His arms went around her and they hugged, taking and giving comfort, mending the wound. Lynn felt a mantle of peace envelop her at last after this wonderful/terrible day. The up-and-down chain of feelings was leveling off, thank heaven. She couldn't have taken much more. No wonder she'd avoided commitment for so long. It was murder. But she was in for the duration now, and she'd have to take the low points with the high.

She pressed her face into Reed's shoulder and he

stroked her hair. He was holding her as if he wanted her never to be in a different room from him again.

He led her to the bed and they lay together. She kissed his neck and snuggled tight against him. It was going to be okay.

Two blue jays squabbling in the maple tree outside her window woke her. She sat up, disoriented. The milky light told her it was a little past dawn; why couldn't she see the clock? Because the other pillow—*Reed's,* she thought with a pang—was bunched up, hiding it. She pulled the pillow away: 6:15.

Embarrassment flooded her. She must have fallen asleep; she couldn't remember anything after they'd lain on the bed in each other's arms.

Straightening the pillow, she touched paper. She turned on the lamp and squinted to read:

> Lovely Lynn,
> Don't feel bad—I went to sleep too. It's 5:30 now and I'm going home to shower and change. Don't make any plans for today—I'll be back at 10. We're going to Portland.
>
> Love,
> R.

Now he was anticipating her on paper. He knew she'd be embarrassed even before she woke up and was. How sweet of him! She felt better. And how nice that he wanted to spend the day with her. But Portland? What could he want to do there?

She'd been ready fifteen minutes early so he wouldn't catch her looking like a war orphan again. "Business or pleasure?" she asked, opening the door.

"I didn't know this was that type of establishment. But if you'd care to get into your leather bikini—"

"I meant Portland."

"Oh, *Portland,*" he said, as though that was the last thing on his mind. "Business. And pleasure. I can't imagine spending a day with you that wouldn't be pleasurable." There was a pause while they both remembered yesterday. Lynn vowed not to lose her perspective again, no matter what the business part turned out to be.

And he was dressed for business, in a lightweight navy blazer over an open-necked striped dress shirt and gray slacks. She was glad she'd dressed for the city, too, in a skirt and heeled sandals.

"Tell me more," she said, turning off a lamp and getting her handbag.

"Better take a jacket. It's supposed to get chilly tonight."

"We won't be back till tonight? Portland's hardly an hour away."

"I thought we'd take our time, see the sights, have dinner."

She locked the door and followed him down. "And?"

He turned around on the stairs and arched his brows suggestively. "And . . . ?"

Her cheeks got warm. "You know what I mean. *And* why are we going there in the first place?"

"You'll see. Just a little idea."

She wasn't sure she liked the sound of that. But they were getting into the car now, and she was distracted by the way the June sun hit Reed's hair, making it shine like copper. Even beneath the jacket she could see his muscles flex as he started the car and backed it out. She remembered how those arms, that big body, had felt last night, and she shivered. What a cretin she'd been to fall asleep!

They headed north to Wells and picked up 95. Reed drove the interstate with authority and finesse. *Just the way he does everything else.* Lynn tried not to watch him, but there wasn't much to look at along the forested highway. And his profile was a work of art, the strong features pensive as he maneuvered the large car. The gray trouser fabric showed the taut lines of his legs. . . . *Oh, somebody throw a bucket of water on this woman with the one-track mind.*

She tried to learn more about why they were going, but he was evasive. So she contented herself with enjoying the ride and his presence next to her, and soon they were off the interstate and heading into downtown Portland.

The sidewalks of the harbor city were full of shoppers and early business lunchers. As they drove past the harbor itself, Lynn saw Roberto's, the ship permanently at anchor that was a restaurant. She knew of it. Mediocre food, but the novelty drew hordes every night.

Reed parked a couple of blocks farther on. He saw Lynn looking around the commercial area curiously and pointed to a store. Downeast Restaurant Supply, she read.

She looked at him, perplexed.

"I made an appointment. Something I'd like you to see."

"A piece of equipment? We always buy from—"

"This is unusual. No other place has it."

She was starting to feel a chill. "Reed—"

"Lynn, look at me." He reached out with both hands and smoothed her hair away from her face. "I brought you here so I could make a suggestion. That's all. Not a demand. Not even a request. Just a suggestion." He kissed her lips, long and gently. "We've had a couple of close calls, letting our conflicts run away with us. You're too important to me to risk losing you over any damn thing. So just remember that. I won't push. The decision is yours."

Her lips still tingling, Lynn preceded him into the showroom. A short, bearded middle-aged salesman approached them.

"Help you folks?" he asked.

"I'm Mr. Graham. I have an appointment with Joe Flannery."

The man grinned. "That's me." He stuck out a fat-fingered hand. "And you wanted to see . . ."

"The convection steamer," Reed said.

"Ahhh," Flannery breathed. "If you folks will just follow me."

He led them down an aisle. The barnlike room was well lighted, but the mammoth restaurant machinery hulked tall on both sides, throwing long shadows that darkened their path. Giant dishwashers, mixing machines, fryers, and ovens lined their way.

"Did you notice his beard bounces when he talks?" Lynn whispered. "And I hate being called a folk. What on earth is a convection steamer?"

"Shh," Reed admonished gently, and she resolved to keep her mouth shut. If he was going to behave, she should too.

They stopped by a double-compartmented device that looked like twin microwave ovens.

"The convection steamer," Flannery said, in the tone he might have used to introduce the Princess of Wales. He looked from Reed to Lynn expectantly.

"Uh-huh," Reed said.

"Very interesting," Lynn said.

"On the phone you mentioned lobsters," Flannery said to Reed, and Lynn looked quickly at him. Lobsters! In a gizmo like this? Their lobsters were boiled in a giant vat of seawater. There was no other way.

"Right," Reed said. "How does it operate?"

"The generator down here in the bottom creates steam, and the lobsters go on these." Flannery opened the doors; racks were inside. "You can fit, oh, ten lobsters on each. So twenty can cook at once. What do you folks think?"

Lynn groaned silently. "Very interesting," she said again, determined to seem openminded.

Reed glanced sideways at her. "What about timing?"

"About the same as if you're boiling—but of course, it's a whole different story from boiling." His sausage hand caressed the fake-wood grain of the steamer as he wound up for his sell. "First of all, you don't have to keep a pot of water going. That means a cooler kitchen and fewer burns. You don't watch the clock. This baby shuts off automatically. The lobster cooks in its own juice, so you don't have water squirting out when the customer cracks it open, getting all over their clothes and all. Heh, heh, heh!" He waited for them to share his enjoyment of the image, and when they didn't laugh, he finished, "And the flavor of a lobster from this—" He kissed his fingertips. "Once you try it, you'll never boil one again."

Lynn was doing her best to look attentive.

"What do you think?" Reed asked her.

"It's very interesting," she said for the third time, wanting to shoot herself. If she was going to play the receptive businesswoman, couldn't she play it with a vocabulary of more than three words?

"If you have any questions . . ." Reed said.

"Anything you want to ask. Anything at all," Flannery chimed in.

Lynn looked from Flannery to Reed and back again. She couldn't take her eyes off the stiff, pointy beard, which bobbed every time the man spoke.

They were waiting for her to ask a question. She had to come up with one. She didn't want Reed to think she'd decided without considering the idea. *Even though you did,* a voice nagged.

"What, uh . . . how do you start it?" she asked, feeling prickles of sweat.

Flannery beamed. "You hit this button that says Start," he said, with no irony.

She had to do better than this. Any minute Reed would realize she was rowing without oars.

"The price!" she said so loudly that Reed jumped, and the salesman eyed her oddly. "How much is it?"

"Fifty-five hundred dollars."

Both men looked at her. Lynn tried to appear as if she was contemplating the purchase, frowning over complex calculations. She made a show of peering inside the cabinets and stooping in back to see the generator.

Finally she said, "I don't know. It's a large outlay. "I'd like to think about it."

"Of course," Reed said immediately. "I just wanted you to have a look."

The salesman walked them to the door, gave them each his card, and waved good-bye, his beard flapping.

"It's a novel idea," Lynn said as they got into the car. "I don't know if it's for us right now, though."

"I understand. No problem at all."

"It *is* good to keep up with what's new. I'm glad you showed it to me. I'd like to sleep on it, maybe talk to Barrie . . ."

"Fine." He started the car. "No rush. Now, how about some sight-seeing? I'd love to look around. Let's be tourists, okay?"

Lynn agreed eagerly. All that courtesy was a strain. On Reed, too, she was sure. It was good to have gotten through a potential battle zone unscathed, but she wanted them to be themselves again.

They spent the afternoon exploring the city, avoiding the overquaint shops and poking instead into the harbor's secret corners. They'd dropped the restrained politeness so naturally Lynn hardly noticed, and the hours went by quickly.

"You have a choice of dining spots," Reed said as they left the harbor parking lot. "Hungry?"

She turned around for a last glimpse of the gulls diving. "Very. Why do they always feed at this hour? Are the fish close to the surface now? Or does it have something to do with the light hitting the water?"

"It's because they've just finished their martinis."

"In other words, you don't know either."

"You don't miss a thing. So let's discuss where the humans are eating. What are you in the mood for?"

"Anything. Seafood, or seafood."

"Think you could narrow it down a little more?"

They smiled at each other. The late-day sun sent peach rays into the car, lighting his face, and his green-gold eyes went translucent. He bent and kissed her lips quickly. The light changed and he stepped on the gas.

"Bad habit," he said.

She turned inquiringly.

"Kissing you at a red light. It's like eating one pistachio nut."

"But your fingers stay cleaner." Her light tone was counterfeit; the kiss had left her longing for more. "Where are we going?"

"I thought Baker's or the Cove."

"Either would be lovely."

"Baker's has that unreal cheese dip. But the Cove has a better parking lot."

"A better . . . ?"

"More private nooks." His grin was radiant.

She laughed to cover her body's reaction. The images his words evoked were making her quiver.

"I'll take your silence as a vote for the Cove."

She started to make a joking retort, but didn't. Of course she wanted to go to the Cove. Why pretend to him, or to herself, that she wasn't dying for the moment when his arms would go around her and his mouth would cover hers?

They left the interstate at Old Orchard Beach and went east to Route 9, the coast road. Lynn's heart pumped faster as they drove into the Cove lot and Reed went past the mosaic of cars parked by the building to a lonely area near the water.

The sun had descended farther, spreading the sea with melted orange. The color rippled as light swells built for their roll toward the beach.

"I never get tired of that," Lynn said. She was exquisitely conscious of Reed's male warmth beside her, but her eyes were on the water. Two delights together. "The sunset never looks the same to me twice."

He brushed a palm over her bare knee. "Like a snowflake."

"Yes," she said, her voice strained. She wished the hand back.

He caught her thought and clasped her knee. "I think a snowflake would vaporize if it got anywhere near us right now, though," he whispered. He moved his hand up slightly. His fingers trailed sparks along her inner thigh.

She wanted more of him. This wasn't the most private spot in the world, but she was rapidly forgetting that in the intimacy of the car as Reed teased her to wild flights with the merest brushes on her skin.

She was overwhelmed with feeling for him. Their day had been great. She felt proud that there'd been no strife over the steamer, glad they'd avoided a childish tug of war. The day itself seemed to symbolize all that had gone before. Tiptoeing around each other's sensibilities . . . finding the common threads, the shared funnybones . . . savoring the surprises of contrasting personalities . . .

And now here they were, so close, the culmination of it all. She knew Reed felt the pull, too, the urge to become lost in a surge of heat.

He lifted her hand and took her little finger in his mouth. His tongue, the silken interior of his cheeks as he pulled on it, were intoxicating. He moved the hand to take in her second finger and let his tongue play in the sensitive pocket between them.

Lynn gasped, a spasm of pleasure shaking her.

Fire was licking through her now. She pulled her fingers from his lips. Foggily surprised at her own aggressiveness, she turned to him, her arms circling his neck, her mouth lifted to receive his. He seemed startled for a moment, and she felt a pang of self-consciousness; but then he responded hungrily, his tongue a sweet invader. Exulting in the special taste of him, she clung to his neck, making no attempt to disguise her yearning. She adored his kisses, the feel of his hands. A river of joy washed over her every time he touched her—or even hinted that he was going to. It was senseless to hide that.

His hands were at her back. He lifted her thin cotton sweater and unfastened her bra. Trying to summon her faraway better judgment, she pulled away to object: they were in public, it wasn't dark yet, anyone could come along. But her lips hadn't formed the first word when he was kissing them again, his own hard and insistent.

He caressed her skin, moving up under the sweater to stroke her shoulders, taking possession of her nakedness. But she pushed his arms down, forcing his hands to her breasts. Now the lightness was gone from his touch. His breathing was heavier. He held the warm softness with a loving strength that set Lynn's blood pounding. She moved under his hands, bolts of desire inflaming her.

Through her mist of pleasure she sensed a change. Something different was happening around them. She looked up; a car had just passed. The setting sun bouncing off the chrome was what had alerted her through eyes lidded with desire. She moved back and pulled down her sweater.

Reed kissed her cheek and swept back her curls to touch his lips to her forehead. "Maybe it's a good thing they came along," he said. "I don't think we knew what planet we were on for a few minutes there." His eyes met hers. "I love you so much I can't function normally when we're together this way. It's like losing my mind temporarily. All I want is to kiss you and hold you more, and . . ." He left it there, but his face said the rest. His eyes still half closed with passion, lips still moist from their kisses, he simply looked at her, staring as if he couldn't get enough of the sight.

She stared back. *He loves me,* she thought. "I love you too," she had to say.

His smile was wide and joyous. They kissed again, gently this time, the relaxed kiss of lovers who have all the time in the world to learn every hidden lagoon of each other's bodies and souls. Lynn started to get out. She needed the briny air on her overheated flesh.

Reed pulled her back. He leaned over her and closed the door. Raising her sweater, he said, "You forgot something." She gasped. She'd almost tried to make a dignified entrance into a crowded restaurant with her bra open. He reached around and did the hooks up for her.

"You didn't even have to look," she whispered.

"Magic hands," he whispered back, and as he drove closer to the restaurant, Lynn thought, *Oh, they surely are.*

CHAPTER SIX

"What do you think?" Reed asked when their entrées had been served.

"The salad has too much chicory, but the dressing is excellent. Vegetables are good. How long do they sauté this spinach, ten seconds? It's lovely. But I wouldn't have done the fish this way."

"No? You can't do much with sea trout."

"Sure you can." She picked critically at it. "Just broiling it with a sprinkle of herbs is lazy. I'd pan-fry it and then deglaze the pan with wine, or even a little liqueur. Of course, we don't serve many things like that at Gull House. As you might have figured out by now."

He frowned. "I think I'm hearing something interesting. Am I imagining it, or are you the caged bird who hasn't had a chance to fly?"

She went back to her fish. "I don't know what you mean."

"Yes, you do," he said, and waited.

The silence lengthened. Lynn scrambled for a way to change the subject.

"And don't try to change the subject," he said

mildly, startling her so that she looked up. Her face must have shown him he'd struck ore.

"So," he said, nodding as his computer put it together, "you want to cook."

She was silent.

He pushed his hair back, and it was the gesture that did it, that and the sight of the little pin she'd put in his glasses. She felt a rush of familiarity, the special trust that was another component of this love that excited her so. She wanted to confide in him. He was so easy to talk to. She'd felt that from the start, even before she'd known she would grow to feel this deeply about him.

"I do want to," she confessed. "I mean, I want to, but . . . I'm not sure I can do it."

"Why not? Who could be better qualified? You've been in the business for years, you obviously have the touch—"

"I don't think I could handle it."

"Handle what?" he asked in genuine bewilderment.

"The pressure. The pace."

He waved that aside. "It's nothing. You don't even notice it after a while."

"For you it's nothing. But that's a big difference between us, Reed. I need to take time working with food. Rushing blows it for me. I'm not comfortable with the pressure in the kitchen."

She looked away. Her experienced eye could see beyond the formal calm of the Cove's elegant paneled dining room to the goings-on behind the kitchen door. In there, she knew, was a cyclone of motion, efficient but frenzied, as the staff hurried to keep up with the orders. And this was only a Tuesday.

"No, change that," she said. "It's the understatement of the decade. I'm terrified of the pressure."

He chewed thoughtfully on a scallop. "Is that really the part you're afraid of, though?"

"Yes! I know it's not a big deal to *you,* but I'm used to a very structured job. It's predictable. There aren't different problems flying at me every time I swallow. I don't need to do nine things at once and have each one come out as if I did it uninterrupted. I'd make a complete fool of myself trying to cook."

He grinned. "Don't you realize what you're saying?"

"No, I don't, and when did you hang out your shingle?" she said, exasperated. "You do the same thing Barrie does. You both know exactly what's on my mind, while I just stumble around in ignorance."

"Sorry. It was so obvious, I didn't see how you could miss it. Just goes to show what experts we are at fooling ourselves. What you did," he went on, "is describe your job to a T. Yes, you do cope with problems flying at you every few minutes. You're always doing a bunch of things at once and making them look effortless. That's *exactly* what you do. You just don't do it in the kitchen."

She was quiet, turning that over in her mind.

"Your job is predictable only because you've been doing it for so long. You know what the crises will be. But there are plenty of them—more than in the kitchen. Lynn, I've seen you with six parties looking at their watches in the reception area, the phone ringing off the hook, and the waitresses needing you constantly in the dining room. You handle all that and clear tables in your spare time. *That's* pressure. It can't be the pressure of the kitchen you dread. I think it must be the change."

"Well, what if it is? That's some change, Reed!"

"No, it isn't! You'll never have that many hassles in the kitchen. It's an oasis of order by comparison. You could handle it fine. And I think you're dying to try."

"I don't know," she said, and sipped her coffee. "Wow. This decaffeinated is better than ours. Let's find out what they use."

"You have to give it a shot," he said, refusing to be sidetracked. "Now. Even though you're scared."

"Why do I?"

"You just have to, that's all. Can't you feel it? It's not right to let your life slide by while you do only safe things that bore you. Come on—you know there's room for an assistant chef."

Her cup was in danger of sloshing. She put it down.

"Not to mention how great it would be to have you in there. To have you near me every night."

That did it. Now she'd never get her cup to her lips without wearing the coffee. "If I did only safe things that bored me," she said, "I wouldn't be here. With you."

"True. And how does it feel? Would you rather be 'safe'—or here with me?"

"Here," she said passionately.

He lifted his cup. "I rest my case."

Someday this will be known as the summer Lynn changed more than her pantyhose, Lynn thought, parking the Chevette at Gull House. She'd spent last weekend showing Antal the ins and outs of hostessing, though the French Canadian waitress whose radar missed nothing already knew the job surprisingly well.

It had taken Lynn three weeks to come around. Objectively she'd known that night at the Cove that Reed was right. But her insides were another matter. Every time she thought of working in the kitchen, she felt as if icicles were climbing her belly. For a while she'd had to put it out of her mind. But when she'd let it back in, a bit at a time, she found she could face it without needing resuscitation.

She'd talked to Barrie. Predictably, her sister had claimed she'd known all along that Lynn secretly wanted to cook.

Finally, with no dodges left, Lynn had decided to hold her breath and dive in. She was nervous, but at least she was willing. And now, with her first night—a placid Wednesday—about to begin, she had to acknowledge another point: courage begat courage. She would never, she thought as she walked across the lot, have dared to try this if she hadn't first tried the relationship. Whatever turmoil her love for Reed had brought to her life, it had also shown her she could step off the curb without getting hit by a truck.

She came through the back door in jeans and an old shirt. Reed did a double-take.

"It's funny seeing you come in empty-handed. No hostess gown," he said.

"No hostess," she answered, and they smiled. "How was lunch?"

"The usual. I guess you survived the dentist."

"It turned out to be just a broken filling. Believe it or not, I was disappointed that I couldn't be here. I wanted to start with a full day."

"I think it's better this way. You're fresh for the main event. Well." He gestured toward the kitchen clothes on hooks near the door. "Put on an apron and we'll get started."

"That's why I wore these. I hate aprons. Will I really need it?"

He peered at her over his glasses. "Do you think I'd wear one if it wasn't excruciatingly necessary?"

"Check." She took one, looped it over her head, and tied it behind her. "Okay. I'm at your service."

"We'd better make some more of the chowders. I figured they'd be slow in this heat, so I didn't make much this morning, but they're almost gone. Should I do that, or do you want to?"

"What do you think?"

He considered. "Well, it's a lot of shucking, steaming, and chopping, but you know how to do them. Maybe I'll leave that to you and I'll make the sauces and stuffings. Keep it uncomplicated for the first day."

"Sounds good," she said. The other cooks were working in their areas; she could see cold platters being garnished with vegetables curled in ice water, and the oven heat was releasing the brown-sugar sweetness of some pecan pies. Everybody seemed to work like lightning. Their hands moved so fast, her eyes could barely follow. Funny; she'd been watching that for years, but never thought much of it. Now that she had to do the same things herself, she felt clumsy. Oh, well, she'd catch on. It was exciting to be part of this, a professional among others, creating edible works of art. After so many years she wouldn't have imagined any part of Gull House could seem so new and different.

She minced salt pork and put it in a pan to render it. When it released enough liquid fat, she'd cook onions in it for the chowder base. *Better steam open the shellfish now to get the broth,* she reminded herself.

"Ow!" she yelled as she dropped a clam into the skillet, splashing hot fat on her hand. Reed was there in a second with ice. He cooled the burn and wrapped gauze around it.

"But it'll get filthy," Lynn said.

"Better than exposing that burn to more heat." He cast an expert eye at her skillet and turned down the flame. "Okay now?"

"Fine. Just embarrassed."

"Don't be. Happens to everyone." He held up his forearms so she could see the undersides. Looking closely, she made out a faint pink-and-white patchwork. "Battle scars," he said. "The mark of a genuine chef. Just think of it as the beginning of your collection."

She smiled and went back to work. The salt pork was almost done, and she started the fish and clams steaming in separate pots. She saw Reed glance at her with amusement and realized she was humming. She was enjoying herself! After all that agonizing, she was actually having a good time, doing what she liked. Why hadn't she tried this years ago?

"Some of the appetizers and vegetables still need to be done," Reed said behind her. His hand rested on her waist. He meant it to be reassuring, she knew, but it just made her breathing quicken. She struggled to keep her attention where it belonged. His sweet breath near her cheek was terribly distracting.

"Someone'll see," she said quietly.

"Let them. Kitchen personnel have to work close together. I'm not doing anything to you I haven't done to Ben or Domenick."

She giggled. "What about the appetizers and vegetables?"

"Which would you rather do?"

"Veggies, I guess. Seems easier than the baked clams and scampi and things."

"Okay. Just remember to keep a timetable in your head, so you don't get thrown when orders start coming."

"Thanks for the hint," Lynn said. "I'm doing fine so far, though. This is easier than I thought it would be. Why was I such a baby?"

"Keep cool. It's still the quiet time. The dinners don't have to be done yet."

She turned back to her chowder preparations. "Damn!" she yelled, whipping the covers off the steaming pots. "I forgot about these." She extracted a clam. "Oh, no! Hockey pucks." Wincing, she poked into the pot with the fish chunks. "This too. You could use them for patio slates. Now I'll have to start over."

"Not really," Reed said. "You can salvage the broth. Just add the celery and potatoes, cook some more fish and shellfish in the separate pots, and you're fine." He looked at his watch. "About an hour till the first order. Better start on the vegetables."

Lynn began preparing broccoli and string beans. Reed saw her laboriously trimming the beans with a knife, and showed her how to do handfuls at a time with shears. But she was so busy with the vegetables that she forgot the fish and clams in the chowder pots, and they toughened again. Too embarrassed to let Reed find out, she surreptitiously removed them from the broth and added still more, determined to time them right. They came out fine. She added cream and butter to the two pots, and put them in the serving area.

The dinner orders were starting. Lynn felt the kitchen gearing up, the staff readying for the accelerated pace. She felt excited too, one of them. It was a little like being a pilot, she decided. You were in charge of many functions at once. You had to do your job right; people were relying on you.

"Why don't you make this order?" Reed said. "Two broiled scallops, two small lobsters. Baked potatoes all around, and you can see the vegetables here." He gave her the slip, and she went at it enthusiastically. Her first complete order!

She scalded herself getting the lobsters out, but the

water burn didn't hurt as badly as the other had, and she bandaged her thumb without anyone noticing. But as she was placing the last of the four plates on the pickup counter, a waitress called, "Eight seafood chowders! Where's the pot?" Lynn froze.

The kitchen noise ebbed suddenly. She felt eyes on her. "I forgot it," she said in a choked voice.

Reed frowned.

"I only made clam and fish," she told him. "The mess-up with the steaming rattled me, I guess, and I forgot to make the third soup."

The waitress grimaced. "That's the most popular one."

"Well, we'll have to do without it for tonight," Lynn said bravely. "Offer them our world-famous clam or fish chowder instead."

Lynn began another order, this one a little more complex. She was adding peppers and onions to a ramekin of shrimp when Reed said, "They're sending back the world-famous chowders."

She turned. "What? All eight?"

"No, more than that. They're all coming back. We can't serve them." He handed her a spoonful. "What kind of a cook doesn't taste?" he asked sternly.

"The kind who doesn't want bacteria in the soup." She sipped and made a face. Inedibly salty!

"You don't have to use the stirring spoon. Just dip another one in. They're both ruined. What the heck did you do, Lynn, pickle the fish first?"

She clapped a hand to her forehead. Her second little mistake that nobody noticed! That meant the soup had triple the usual saltiness—more, in fact, because the two oversteamings had left an even greater concentration of salt.

Her limbs felt cold, as though freezing water ran in her veins. Panic was stealing over her. What *had* she gotten herself into?

Her voice faltering, she explained what had happened, the hidden mistakes.

Reed scowled. "Well, we'll have to do without chowder tonight, unless I get a chance to make some. You'll need to take over some of my work if I do, of course."

"No!" Lynn choked.

"Lynn . . ."

"You don't know how I feel."

"I do know. But you have to put it behind you."

"I've never felt so—so exposed. I made a bunch of little mistakes, and some of them added up to one bozo of a mistake, and now the whole staff can see how inept I was. And I can just imagine what the customers think. No chowder! I must have been crazy to think I could be a chef. I'm mortified!"

"You don't have time to be mortified. We're heading into the busy hours now. We've got to move."

She'd lost all track of time. She was sure that, if she looked outside, she'd see dawn breaking. "Heading *into* the busy hours?"

"Of course," he said, peering at her as if she'd sprouted whiskers. "It's only six forty-five."

She groaned. "I thought this was going to be an uneventful Wednesday night."

"This *is* an uneventful Wednesday night. The only thing making it eventful is you." He cupped her face in his palms and looked straight into her dark eyes. "You can do this, Lynn, I know you can. It's confusing at first; you just have to try and stay organized." He kissed her nose, a swift peck. "Let's do some cooking, Ms. Chef, okay?"

She felt a little better. Some of the staff were eyeing them, others were pointedly not looking, but she paid no attention. She and Reed would get through this together.

With renewed determination she plunged back into the order. She got her hand full of Newburg sauce and then accidentally smeared it in her hair when she reached behind her for a towel. Resolutely, she made herself ignore the mess.

"Have to watch you every minute," she heard Reed mutter a few minutes later. "These are backward."

"What are?"

"It was supposed to be shrimp Newburg, and crabmeat with peppers and onions. You did it the other way around."

She wondered frantically how to fix it, scanning the kitchen as if the answer would appear out of a cabinet, like a jack-in-the-box.

"There's nothing you can do," Reed said. "Just put them aside and start over. Someone will eat them later."

She left them on an unused counter and started again, studying the waitress slip carefully this time. That order done at last, she went on to the next. She'd heard Beth shout it out, but had been too busy to remember it. So many details at once! Now she bit her lip impatiently as she tried to decipher Beth's crabbed handwriting.

"What the hell," she shouted finally, "is 'fou flor'? Or 'stirp'? Am I supposed to be an archaeologist now? I'm here to cook, not decipher heiroglyphics!"

"Let me see," Reed said. He needed only a second. "Fou flor is flounder Florentine. Stirp is striped bass."

"You say that as if I wasn't able to make 'cat' out of c-a-t!" Lynn yelled.

"Just takes practice," he said. "Simmer down, will you? We've got a ways to go."

They both turned sharply as a pot of lobsters boiled over, sending seawater cascading across the burners with a loud hiss.

"Yours?" Reed yelled as they dived for the gas jets. "Of course. Why do I even ask? Lizzie Borden strikes again. Go check the orders and see what you can trash next while I try to get the stove cleaned, or we won't be able to use these burners at all."

Furiously she shook water and lobster froth off her shirt sleeve.

"You got me in the eye," a passing dishwasher said.

"Sorry," she hissed through clamped teeth. "I was aiming for Oz the great and powerful over here. If you don't mind," she said bitingly to Reed, turning to where he knelt by the stove, "I'd like to do my other orders myself. I don't want a watchdog. Go woof at somebody else. If I make a mistake, I'll take the consequences."

"Look, Lynn, I'm sorry I lost my temper, but—"

"Sautéed lobster, broccoli, rice on the side," a waitress called, "and bouillabaisse, no mussels."

"No mussels?" Lynn wailed. "That's like tying your shoes with no laces."

"We can't sauté yet," Reed said from below.

"Ugh, that's right. Say there'll be a slight delay, and give them a drink on the house," she told the waitress. She flipped through the slips and found one that needed no stovetop work. She prepared the broiled fish, and assembled the bouillabaisse for the other order while they cooked. But she lost track of time, and the broiled items burned. She put them aside, quickly did more, and then sautéed the lobster, since Reed had the stove working again.

The lobster and bouillabaisse were ready simultaneously, a bit of dexterity she was congratulating herself for when one of the waitresses said, "What's taking so long? Eighteen has been waiting half an hour for their dinners."

"The stove burners were out," Lynn said, "and we had to—"

"These are broileds. Could you check?"

Reed appeared behind her, his practiced fingers running through the slips. "Haven't you been taking them in order?"

"I took the first one that didn't need a burner."

"The first one on top? That's last. You work from the back. Here's the one she means. You get that while I—"

"Since when? We've always worked from the top."

"Since I took over the kitchen. All the best restaurants—"

"Don't be patronizing. We *are* a best restaurant!'

"We won't be," Reed shot back, "if we don't get it together in here! With one bomb after another leaving this kitchen, we'll be lucky if there isn't a mob storming the place with clubs!"

"Look, I know I haven't risen to Master Chef Graham's standards of perfection, but I'm doing all right. I'm not exactly a beginner, you know. I've been in this business—"

"The sautéed lobster was supposed to have the rice on the side," the other waitress said, pushing through the swinging door with the plate, "and he says he won't pay fifteen fifty for a bowl of bouillabaisse that small."

"Of course the bouillabaisse is small!" Lynn shouted. "He didn't want mussels in it! What was I supposed to fill it out with, bottle caps? And you can just scrape off the stupid rice, put the lobster in another dish, and bring more rice on the side. I don't see why—"

Reed clapped a hand over her mouth. While she struggled under it he said quietly, "Calm down. We're both going to have ulcers if we keep on like this." Holding his hand in place, he told the waitress, "Tell the customer the bouillabaisse will be ten dollars." To Lynn, "We have to do the lobster over. If you try a patch job they can always tell, and it looks bad for us. It isn't worth the ill will." He took his hand away. "We'll get through this. I promise."

Beth burst into the kitchen. "That's not wine sauce on the striped bass! I clearly wrote . . ."

Lynn sprawled across a chair, wrung out. It was eleven; the kitchen had just officially closed and the cleanup was starting.

"There's a banquet here," a cook said, pointing to the counter where Lynn's mistakes were piled.

Reed looked at the heaps of seafood-laden plates and whistled. "Never, not even in my earliest—"

"Oh, shut up," Lynn said wearily. "We'll make soup out of it or something."

"Were you planning to invite the Lions Club? Because there's enough—"

"Reed," she said warningly.

He came over and gazed fondly down at her. "I'm just trying to cheer you up." He smiled. "Look at you. The lady who didn't think she'd need an apron. You should have had a wet suit."

"Oh, no." She was so worn out, she hadn't given a thought to the sight she must have presented. The evening's accidents ran through the Moviola in her mind.

She pulled herself out of the chair, went to the mirror by the bathroom—and shrieked. She looked like the victim of a particularly complex accident. Dirty bandages trailed from a hand and an arm; her hair was matted with dried sauce. Half her clothing was wet, most of it was speckled with a vast array of multicolored spots, and her sneakers looked like the floor of a filling station.

She put her hands over her face. Reed pulled them away.

"Actually," he said, "you're dressed just fine for the after-work activity I had in mind."

"What's that? Washing the Dumpster?"

"Not quite," he said, his eyes a caress, and in spite of the awful night, their bursts of temper, and her bedraggled appearance, Lynn was captured immediately. She was his however he wished.

"I knew tonight would be tense, so I planned a way for us to unwind. I'm sorry I lost it a few times there . . ."

"Well, me too, I wasn't exactly . . ."

"You had a reason; it was your first time. I should have stayed calmer. I should have helped you more. Will you meet me out back in twenty minutes?"

She would have met him in Sri Lanka. She dragged herself to her dressing room, scrounged up clean jeans and a top, and changed. She ached for a shower, and her long-sleeved shirt was too hot for the steamy night, but she was glad to shed the filth-stiffened outfit she'd worked in.

Reed was waiting for her by the Dodge, in that pose she remembered so well—leaning back, with his torso pushed provocatively forward. Now that she knew those contours intimately, the position was more enticing than ever.

She asked where they were going as he pulled out of the parking lot.

"Take a look." He gestured at the backseat. She leaned over and saw two sleeping bags.

"I don't know if the outdoors is as tranquilizing for you as it is for me," he said, guiding the Dodge away from town, "but I thought this was just what we'd need tonight."

"A campout?" she asked doubtfully.

"Graham style." He grinned.

"I'm afraid to ask."

"Relax. You'll love it," he said, and soon he'd turned off the road and they were moving slowly along a rutted dirt track in pine woods.

Lynn was quiet, enjoying the sharp smell, the insects' singing. He parked and handed her one of the sleeping bags. They set off through the pines. There was enough starlight so they could move without tripping over the trees' shallow roots. Fallen needles made soft footing.

Finally they came to a clearing, and Lynn realized that a new noise had joined that made by the insects: a rushing stream. It looked cool and inviting. The night was so muggy that they were sweating from the short hike.

They put down the sleeping bags and Reed stepped close and hugged her. "I felt for you tonight," he said.

Her arms tightened around him. "It was the pits."

"The worst is over."

"Can I believe that?"

"Yes." He buried his face in her hair. "And may I say something else?"

"What?"

"You smell like fish and cooking grease."

She thwacked his back. It was all she could reach.

"If you had let me go home and shower, I wouldn't be offending your delicate nostrils."

"Oh, but we're going to take care of that."

"You're bringing me home?" Disappointment prickled.

"No." He was unbuttoning her shirt. "I'm bathing you."

"You're—in there?" she asked, pointing at the brook.

"I don't see any marble bathtubs, do you?"

"Won't it be cold?"

"Yes." He unzipped her jeans and pushed them down over her hips, caressing as he went. The feathery strokes on her pelvic bones, above her bikini panties, made her shiver. When his hands reached the satin flesh of her thighs, it was all she could do to stay upright. She began to tremble harder.

He helped her step out of the jeans. "You're very suggestible," he said softly. "Just hearing that the water will be cold is making you shiver." He wrapped her in his arms, rubbing her back as if to soothe the tremor away.

"It's not that. It's you."

Her confession seemed to inflame him. His arms tightened like steel cable around her as his mouth found hers. The taste of him, the thrilling pressure of his hold, sent showers of delight along every nerve in Lynn's body. She kissed him back with abandon, her bikinied hips thrusting to meet him, to feel the throb of his yearning for her.

But before the kiss could carry them both beyond

the here and now, Reed stepped back, still holding her. Reluctantly Lynn dropped her arms from his neck. The feel of the brawn beneath his shirt was tempting, and she let her hands linger on his biceps, her thumbs tracing the contours of muscle through the thin fabric.

"Ready?" he asked quietly. She noticed that his breathing was uneven, and hers quickened again as if in response. Impulsively she buried her face in his neck. She bit at the flesh under his jawbone, feeling the cat's-tongue scratchiness of his late-day beard.

"We're never going to get you washed if you don't cut that out," he said, gripping her face and pulling her back.

"Can't you stand me the way I am?"

"I could stand you covered with motor oil."

"Then . . . ?"

"Trust me."

He moved away and undid his belt, and she finally got the picture: he meant for them to wash together in the stream. *Dingbat, what did you expect? That he'd dip you in like a sock?* Just another example of her sharply limited ability to put one cell in front of the other and cogitate rationally in his presence.

He'd removed his shirt and was starting on his pants. She looked hard, felt a jab of embarrassment, and raised her eyes. She felt his gaze on her, watching her reaction intently as he unzipped his pants and began to push them down.

Probably if he hadn't been staring that way, reading her feelings so clearly, she would have been able to force away her sudden shyness. But in that second she felt a rush of the old terror of giving away a part of herself; and instead of watching the exciting spectacle unfolding before her, she turned away. She gazed into the aromatic blackness of the pine forest and tried to gather back her courage, her confidence as a woman loving and loved. Then Reed said, "Turn around, Lynn," and something in his voice made her obey.

He was nude. His big body was lighted by the moon's soft glow. He stood with his feet slightly apart, reaching for her. He was an intoxicating sight. It was as close to heaven as Lynn had ever been. The outdoor symphony, the stream's fresh smell . . . and powerful arms ready to embrace her under the stars, the arms of a man with whom she shared a splendid love—and whom she wanted now with every thread of her soul.

He hugged her close, then led her to the stream. He stepped into the tumbling waist-deep water and pulled her in, sensing her hesitation, wordlessly coaxing her past it. His hands on her, he felt her small shudder at the chill, and he squeezed her in reassurance.

Three things occurred to Lynn simultaneously: the water wasn't as icy as she'd expected; its current, scary when she'd first eyed it, felt no stronger than a firm caress; and the combination of the swirling water and Reed beside her was incredibly sensuous.

"Cold?" he asked.

"No. It feels wonderful. I've never done anything like this."

He leaned over and took her earlobe in his mouth, bit it softly, released it. He kept his hands maddeningly to himself. "Glad you came?"

"Oh, yes," she breathed.

He took soap and a washcloth from the bag he'd placed by the stream. He lathered her skin slowly, using the cloth and his hands. The soap smelled foreign, exotic, perfect for now. He washed her, every inch, his fingers smooth in the lather, gliding silkily about, over and under. He soaped her hair and eased her down to rinse it. Lynn could feel the clear water carrying off the grime of the evening, and with it the tension and the vestige of fearful shyness that had briefly returned tonight. The suds swirling away on the current took all Lynn's fears and doubts, leaving only the two of them, a pair of lovers alone with the woods and the stars.

"I want to," Lynn said as Reed began to wash himself. She took the soap. Her blood was racing like the swift water, fired by the all-over intimacy of his lather-smoothed hands. She wanted her turn, the chance to map his contours with her fingers.

She started with his chest, soaping the auburn curls. She massaged the bulging pectoral muscles and watched his eyes narrow and his breathing increase as her palms moved back and forth across his nipples. She slid sudsy fingers under his arms, then behind to wash his back. Her breasts brushed his chest and he tried to pull her nearer, but the pleasure of washing him was so intense that she moved away and went around him to continue.

She soaped his broad back, rubbing along the nubs of his spine, up to his neck and down again. She took her time, not wanting the treat to end. She sensed she wouldn't be able to move much lower without pushing him beyond the brink. And she was right: when her hands dropped to savor the beginning roundness of his buttocks, he gave a gasp that was nearly a cry, turned, and wrapped her in his arms.

He was still so soapy that their bodies wriggled together in a slippery clutch of passion. Their hands moved over each other, all pretense of washing gone. Reed pulled away just enough to caress her breasts, and his insistent fingertips tormented her, lifting her to a pitch of near-delirium.

She was aching for him, and she told him so with her hands, desire making her bold. For a moment it seemed he'd have her right there in the water, and she didn't care; she'd have gone along joyously no matter where or how. The burning that had started deep inside when she'd looked at him standing nude had melted through every fiber to consume her. Only the total blending of their bodies in the love that engulfed them would satisfy her.

But then she felt him pull away, the tautening of his muscles showing what an effort it was. She struggled to fit herself back into his arms, but he lifted her out of the water. He lowered her onto the grass-cushioned bank and lay beside her.

"Can't we—I want—" She reached for him, but he quieted her with a quick kiss.

"Soon. I want to love you some more," he said, and rolled her onto her stomach.

His big fingers kneaded her back in long strokes, lubricated by the water. Gradually the burning subsided to a delicious tingle. She felt she could lie there on the stream bank forever, being kissed and petted. He murmured to her, soothing sounds and words of passion. She hadn't imagined, earlier, that she could ever feel this relaxed again.

Then she slowly became aware of a difference, of her body's thermostat beginning to peak once more. He was stroking her in another way, she realized through her fog of pleasure: firmly massaging her calves and thighs, now her derrière. Instantly she was back at the fierce pitch of yearning she'd reached when he made them wait. She rolled over so abruptly that they both tumbled back into the stream.

They surfaced with their arms around each other. *No more waiting, it's happening now,* Lynn thought, and immediately she found herself standing in the water with her back against the bank pressing the wet tufts of greenery there as Reed moved to unite them at last.

She cried out when the whole size and strength of him became part of her. Again he was whispering, the words broken by his passion. The flow of love sounds in her ear matched the rhythm she'd found with him, the ecstatic motion of their joining, and Lynn was transported up and up, beyond consciousness.

His arms tightened, gripping her harder. The blinding star shower was on them both. The surge of the water, the rush of their passion, were one force. An endless aching moment of nearly unbearable joy . . . and then Lynn was falling gently back to earth, safe in Reed's arms, more loved than she'd ever been, than anyone had ever been.

CHAPTER SEVEN

"Good night. No, leave it open, thanks," Lynn told the dishwasher who was closing the door.

"Well, that's it," Reed said. "Nobody left but us owls." He brought two cups of coffee to the kitchen table, where she was sitting. "There's a little brandy in it. Good for what ails you."

She sipped. Her big dark eyes were morose. "Why am I still so tense, when I've been cooking for a month? Will I ever get used to it?"

"Yes. Next question."

She was silent, trying to relax.

"Okay, I'll ask one. How do you like the coffee?"

"It's nice. Why do I get a china cup, when I gave you the whole production in a goblet? Wow, was that only a couple of months ago? It seems like a century."

"That's because you've spent half of it charging into battle, dodging grenades and land mines."

She smiled. "When you put it that way, I don't feel like such a chicken."

"No reason you should at all. This is a big adjustment. Based on my limited knowledge of you"—she raised her eyebrows, and he flashed his golden smile, but pushed on—"I've picked up a hint that change isn't your strong suit. Would you say that's accurate?"

"Oh, I don't know. Just because it takes an act of Congress to get me to wear a new lipstick . . ."

"Even if that wasn't an issue with you, starting as a chef would be frightening. It took forever before I stopped wanting to enter a kitchen with a false mustache and an alias. And I *like* to experiment. You deserve a double pat on the back." He sipped his coffee and grimaced. "And a decent cup of coffee. Beth must have made the last pot without getting rid of what was in there. This is swill. Why didn't you tell me it was so bad?"

Lynn shrugged. "I didn't notice."

"You *must* be shellshocked. This stuff could eat through brass. Here, give me that, I'll make fresh."

"No, don't bother." She got wearily out of her chair. "Thanks, but I think I'll just go home and collapse."

"Stay a minute." He took her hand. "I'd like to talk about something."

Lynn sat, curious in spite of her fatigue.

"I've been thinking I'd like to buy in," he said, his eyes intent on hers, "if you and Barrie are willing."

Lynn was still. She was amazed to realize her heart was hammering. The idea was out of the question, of course. She and Barrie were partners. Co-owner of Gull House, that was her job. Three owners would be too many. It would cause confusion, and—well, it was out of the question, that was all.

Her face must have hinted at her thoughts, because Reed put in hastily, "Not a full third. I know what you and Barrie went through to build this place, and I don't want to muscle in. But, Lynn, try to see it from where I sit."

She would simply say no. He'd accept that; he had to. Or maybe she wouldn't just yet. She'd appear to think awhile, pretend she hadn't rejected the idea outright.

"You look," he said, "as if you have no intention of even listening to my reasoning." He took off his glasses and cleaned them with a napkin. He pushed his hair back and replaced them. "Your whole attitude says you want me to go away and take my lousy idea with me."

Unconsciously Lynn was gripping her chair seat. She felt transparent, naked. He'd seen right through to her terror of losing even a little piece of Gull House. He hadn't said it quite that way, but then, how could he know the full extent of her fear? She hadn't herself until now. As with so many things that spring from deep within the heart, she'd had no idea how strongly she felt until the danger was smack in front of her.

"Do you realize you haven't said a word in about five minutes?" he asked, his eyes scanning her face.

"Uh, yes," she said. If she looked half as dazed as she felt, no wonder he was getting nervous. *What's wrong with me?* she wondered frantically. *I must be nuts, so neurotically attached to Gull House that I feel sick to think of losing a corner of it. Is that the only way I define myself, by this place I created? Here I am planning to lie to this man who's so honest, who loves me . . . to pacify him so he'll go away and take his lousy idea with him—just like he said.*

"Earth to Lynn." He passed a hand back and forth in front of her face. "Is it so unreasonable? Just give me a chance to make my case, huh?"

The words were gentle, but a determination shaded them, a message she oughtn't to ignore. Somewhere she knew he wasn't being unreasonable; she was. But she was scared, so scared . . . it was hard to see the situation as it really was. She knew she'd at least better listen, though. Whatever steel control it took, she had to give him his say.

"Okay," she told him, lightening her voice as convincingly as she could, "let's hear the whole idea. I'm sorry if . . . I mean, it was just a surprise, that's all."

There was that beloved grin, lighting the green-gold eyes that haunted her days and her dreams. "I didn't mean to scare you. I guess you feel like I leaped in here with a mask and said, 'Your restaurant or your life.' "

She managed a thin smile.

"I just want to be . . . more settled, I guess is the best way to put it." He ran a finger along the back of her hand where it rested on the table, clenched. "A certain lady seems to be having that effect on me. See, I've spent my whole career refining my techniques and I'm ready for them to start paying dividends. But I'm still working for a salary."

His face implored her to understand, and she made herself stay quiet and let him talk.

"I don't want to be a paid employee. I want to be an investor. Investing my talent, sharing the expenses, seeing some of the results of my work. Working along with you and Barrie to help build something that's a little bit mine."

"Build?" she repeated, not sure what he meant.

He chuckled. "Don't look so nervous. I mean in small, basic ways, good business moves. Expanding into that extra wing, maybe," he said, waving toward the room they used for storage. "Automating more routines, like the coffee making, so we don't wind up at the end of the night serving something that tastes like it came from the bottom of a crankcase."

Lynn made herself nod reasonably. "I'd like to think about it," she said.

"That's fine. Chew on it. Talk to Barrie. I don't expect you to be enthusiastic right off, but I think you'll see it my way once you give the idea a chance." He squeezed her hand. "Sometimes you come to a point in your career when you know it's time for a leap. Like you did, starting in the kitchen. What's happening in your personal life can be a factor. I know that's part of it with me. I didn't think I'd be ready to invest for a few years yet. But you've made me feel things that I. . . . Well," he trailed off, looking sheepish, "I guess I shouldn't load too much on you at once."

He came around the table as she stood. The kitchen's steamy heat had made her glossy black hair form ringlets that brushed her shoulder. He pulled them aside and kissed her neck.

"I love you," he said. "I'm glad you listened. Now

you look like you need a good long sleep. I'll walk you out."

Lynn gave the pan of oatmeal a stir and set out a bowl and spoon. Sun streamed into her compact kitchen, shining from the carefully waxed floor, but she barely noticed.

Isn't it time you returned to the land of the humans? she asked herself. It had been nearly a week since Reed's polite question that had struck her like a dart. She'd hashed it out in her head, shaken it in her teeth, thrown it in the air, tried it on for size, made herself face the panic it created.

She'd phoned Barrie the next day, before work, and told her about Reed's request—quite casually, she thought. But her sister hadn't been fooled.

"You're hoping I'll refuse to sell any of my half," she'd said promptly.

"Hoping? That's ridiculous. Why would I—"

"So you'll have an excuse to say no. It doesn't take ESP to figure that out from everything you've told me. He wants to buy a piece, you don't want to let him, but you don't want to lose him either. My guess is that it's been hard enough for you to give part of yourself; look at the years you spent avoiding that. You can't bring yourself to give up a hunk of Gull House too. You want me to get you off the hook."

"That's an interesting way of looking at it."

"In other words, you know I'm right, but you'll eat thumbtacks before you'll admit it."

Lynn sighed. "All right. Let's pretend—"

"You got it. Fairy tale time. Go on."

"Stop it. This is important. Let's pretend for a minute that you're right. What would be the best thing to do?"

"Beats me."

Lynn waited. Then, "That's it?"

"Yup."

"Come on, Barrie. Where's your Dr. Brothers imitation now that I need it?"

"You only think you need it. The answers are in *your* head. The decision can only come from you."

"But I've helped you out on things like this. Remember when you were getting ready to marry John, and you had doubts? Didn't I stay up a whole night with you, talking it out? We were like zombies the next day. And we had to work."

"That was different. Prewedding jitters. Everybody has them."

"Oh, is that so? You weren't so cavalier at the time."

"Of course not. I was in the problem at the time. Just like you are now. Lynn, all I can say is that I'll make part of my half available for sale if you want me to—but I can't help you decide what to do with your part of the place, or with any parts of yourself."

Now, eating her cereal, she wrestled with the question yet again. Gull House was her baby, hers and Barrie's, and she loved it with the mother-wolf ferocity she'd feel if it were a real child. She loved it as it was, the way they'd raised it. She saw no reason to change it. Wasn't it superb now?

Reed had said his wish to buy in was tangled with his feelings for her. He'd talked about settling down.

She poured more coffee and watched a yellowjacket investigating the maple leaves by the kitchen window. The idea was tantalizing, she had to admit. She loved Reed; she knew in her viscera that he loved her. She didn't need constant reassurance. It radiated from his every action and word. But if the price of permanence was that she'd have to share Gull House, see it shift and change . . .

And yet again, she asked herself whether she wasn't seeing the threat as more than it was. An armed attack, rather than a new direction. What did she expect, when she and Reed were as different as honey and garlic? Wasn't that a big part of their attraction? His flamboyance excited her; he respected and admired her stability. She'd been trying harder to accept his ways, just as he'd been more patient with hers.

She cleared away the breakfast things, did the dishes, and dressed for work. She might still be having a rough time as a cook, she reflected as she started the car, but one thing about her new career was a treat: no more gowns. They were so elegant—but such a pain.

She parked next to Reed's Dodge, the only car in the lot. Good—they'd have a few moments alone before the others started arriving. She went up the back steps and into the kitchen—and stopped dead. Astonishment turned immediately to outrage.

"What is that?" she asked Reed, furiously biting off each word, though she could see only too well what it was: the convection steamer she'd seen in Portland.

Reed had just uncrated the machine and was rolling it toward the wall. "Isn't it beautiful? Now we can—"

"Where do you get the nerve?" Lynn yelled. "How dare you try to push me like this? You asked if you could buy in—I haven't even given you an answer yet, much less authority to buy equipment!"

"Lynn!" He gripped her trembling shoulders. He was smiling. "It's a surprise. I paid for it myself." He stepped back and folded his arms, ready to bask in her delight.

"You *what?* That's the sneakiest thing I ever heard." She began to pace the kitchen, her fury rising with every step. "Of all the rattlesnake moves—"

"No, you have it all wrong," Reed said, following her. "I did it to show my good faith. I couldn't wait for you to get here and see the thing. I thought you'd be thrilled."

"No, you didn't. You're trying to force the issue. Capture more and more territory, put your money in, behave like a partner, so that eventually we have no choice but to make you one. That's *pressure,* Reed, like a loanshark or something!"

Furious as she was, she knew she'd gone too far when she saw Reed's face color immediately.

"A loanshark? Are you nuts? Do you even know what you're talking about? All I do is buy a new piece of machinery for your precious restaurant, to show you how I'm willing to commit myself—and you call me a criminal!" He slapped the top of the steamer. "What would you do if I bought you a piece of jewelry? Have me arrested?"

"You're putting words in my mouth! I didn't—"

"Any I'm putting in have to be better than the ones I'm hearing! How would you like it if I called you something like that?"

"That isn't the point! You're making a smokescreen out of one stupid word that happened to slip out!"

"It couldn't have slipped out if it hadn't been in there in the first place! What the hell do you think of me? I thought you loved me!"

"I do love you!" she shouted back, and just at that moment a cook walked in, stopped whistling, looked at Lynn's face, then Reed's, and turned and left.

Flushing hotly, Lynn went to the door. "It's okay, Ben," she called. "Just a little difference of opinion." She heard Reed's strangled cough behind her. "Come on in."

Lynn was half tempted to slam out of there and let Reed cope by himself, but she resisted the unprofessional impulse and got to work as the rest of the team filtered in. Her hands still shook with anger. Quick glances at Reed told her he was livid, too, trying to deal politely with the staff and succeeding, but just barely.

Barrie came into the kitchen. "Hi, everybody," she said. "About time we got rid of that heat wave, huh?" She noticed the steamer. "What's this?"

"Yeah, I meant to ask about that," a cook said.

There was a long silence, during which only the clink and clatter of kitchen tools could be heard.

At last Lynn said, "It's a convection steamer."

"A what?" Barrie asked.

"A convection steamer!" Lynn hissed through clenched teeth.

"What's it for?"

"Well, that's the big question, isn't it?" she shouted. Every head in the room swiveled in Lynn's direction. " '*Who* is it for?' would be even better. But don't waste your time asking me. Ask the man who bought it!" she finished, pointing a shaking finger at Reed.

"Are you going to make this public now?" Reed fired back. "I've had about enough of—"

"What in heaven's name is going on?" Barrie interrupted, hands on her small hips. "Is this the Security Council? I walk in and ask a simple question, and get caught in a crossfire."

Lynn turned back to her chopping block and angrily sliced shrimp, embarrassed by her outburst but still seething.

"Sorry," Reed said shortly, and returned to the stove.

Barrie looked from one to the other, shrugged, and left the kitchen. Slowly voices began to fill the heavy quiet as talk resumed. Most of the staff were old pros, used to the occasional chef tantrum. Of course, these fights between the chef and Lynn weren't quite your garden variety kitchen spat. But it seemed the show was over for today, anyway.

Lynn took the last four entrées out of the oven. It had been a long day. She and Reed were speaking only when necessary, confining their conversation to work. But her anger had pretty much evaporated. The dinnertime hassles had pushed it aside. Would she ever learn to take all the kitchen emergencies in stride?

And she wasn't blameless herself. Maybe he'd been deceptive and maybe not; he might only have wanted to show his good faith, as he claimed. But he'd had every right to expect she'd keep an open mind about the steamer when she saw it in Portland—and she hadn't. She'd never considered buying it. She'd only pretended. He must know that now. Obviously, she hadn't even bothered to discuss the machine with Barrie.

"Two compliments on the sole special," a waitress shouted from the doorway, and Lynn smiled. The dish was her creation. The fillets were baked under a lemon-lime-orange butter. She was especially proud of the garnish, thin rounds of the three fruits fanned into an artful design.

Reed gave her thumbs-up with a big, slow grin. After a moment she grinned back.

"Peace?" he asked.

She nodded, feeling a wave of relief, and then they both spoke at once.

"I know you meant well with the—"

"We don't have to keep the—"

"—steamer," they finished together, and laughed.

"Let's forget about the whole issue for now," Reed said. "What do you think?"

"I think that's a spectacular idea."

"What should we talk about instead?"

Lynn tore her eyes from the silky hair falling across

his glasses, the open neck of his shirt where a patch of auburn teased her. "About cleaning up, I guess."

"Oh, yeah, that." He took plastic wrap and began gathering pieces of fish that were still out. Lynn put away the sauces, stealing peeks at Reed as he worked. She tried not to be obvious. The kitchen's noise level let them speak normally without being overheard, so as long as they didn't shout, their conversation was private in the crowded room; but eyes were another matter.

She knew she was noticed watching Reed, but she had no intention of stopping. Every sight was a joy. The artistry in his hands, the sinews working in his chest and shoulders when he disjointed a huge lobster or filleted a whole fish . . . the powerful legs stretched out as he crawled behind machinery to fix it.

Finally the last dishwasher left. "Coffee? A little liqueur?" Reed asked. "And then how about a drive along the coast road?"

"Sure," Lynn said quickly. How much better it felt to speak this way to Reed rather than try to do battle with him. "Want my brandy and tequila coffee?"

"The kind you made when we met? The bribe-a-chef special?"

"Bribe? Oh, right. I was trying to entice you into taking this undesirable spot, this depressing job in a dirty, urban, crime-ridden—"

"Okay, okay. I was pulling your beautiful leg. Actually, I would have bribed you to let me stay. Now, how about that coffee?"

While she assembled it, she asked, "Did you say that just so I'd make the coffee?"

"What would you do if I said yes?"

"I'd make it anyway."

"Really? That's sweet."

"And then I'd pour it in your lap. Here, taste." She gave him the sugar-frosted stemmed glass. "Enough brandy?"

"Perfect."

They sat in friendly silence. "Let me go clean up a little," Lynn said after a few minutes, "and then we can take a ride. I feel dirty and sticky." She rose and took her glass. "How come you still stay so much cleaner than I do?"

"Just general superiority." She threw a napkin at him. "And a bigger apron. Hurry back."

She climbed the winding stairs and turned on the light in her dressing room. The soft glow from the wall sconces illuminated the velvet loveseat and crimson shag carpet. An oval mirror above her vanity table reflected the red, black, and gold flower print of the wallpaper, enlarging the cozy room.

She took off her sandals and slacks and pulled her shirt over her head. She went to work with a wash-cloth and soap in the little bathroom and in a few minutes felt fresh again.

She checked her face in the mirror, flicked away a stray speck of mascara, and finger-combed her thicket of curls. In her panties she went to the closet to get clean clothes.

"So this is your sanctum," Reed said from the door,

and she spun around to find him standing there, holding his coffee glass, looking her over with obvious pleasure.

Her impulse was to grab something from the closet to hide herself. Then she nearly laughed out loud at how inane that was. After all . . .

"I was hoping I'd catch you this way," he said, not even making a pretense of averting his eyes. He came to her and gazed into her face for a long moment before bending to kiss her lips softly. His hand moved with infinite gentleness along her waist. His tongue entered her mouth to find hers, electrifying her. Flame shot to her toes.

He touched her cheek as he pulled his lips away.

"It was this," he said, indicating his coffee glass, which he placed on the vanity. "It reminded me of that night. The taste . . . it brought everything back in Technicolor. I was sitting in the kitchen just now, and all I could think of was"—he kissed her again, his lips a loving pressure—"all I could think of was what I wanted to do that night. What you made me feel, how exciting you were."

Lynn said, "But that was the first—"

"The first day we met. It didn't matter. From the first minute, all I could think of was you. Your hair, your face—the way your eyes look, as if everything is amusing you. Even after we fought, even after I tore out of here and swore I'd never come back—I knew that wasn't how it would be. In just that one day, I felt things I'd never . . ."

He kissed her once more, then moved up along her

jaw to her ear, nibbling the lobe, leaving little kisses all along her hairline.

"That night," he whispered, "I almost had to sit on my hands to keep myself from . . . this."

He pulled her to him. She gripped his shoulders, holding him as tightly as he held her, meeting his lips. His hands dropped to her derrière, molding, pressing. The heat that flowed through her veins made her forget everything, where they were, everything, and she dropped her own hands and clasped him the same way, pulling him to her with equal urgency.

She was aware of nothing but her yearning for him, and without knowing she was going to do it, Lynn pushed him to the loveseat. With passion-heavy fingers she started to take off his shirt. He helped her, in a hurry too, and when the shirt was off she reached for his belt. Her hands were fumbling, inexpert, hampered by her desire. He must have helped her there as well, because in a few tremulous seconds his slacks were off and he was before her on the loveseat.

The hunger Lynn felt was immense, born of her love, and instinct guided her. She felt Reed's hands on her shoulders and face, and in her hair. Never in her life had she known such a craving for a man, but Reed . . . Reed was magic. She wanted to know him as intimately as it was possible to know a man, to show her passion completely, to give him as much pleasure as possible and to take from him all that he could give.

There was a second when he opened his eyes and stared heavy-lidded at her. His expression was half rapture, half surprise, as if confirming that these love-emboldened hands and lips really belonged to his Lynn. But then he was being carried far off.

His cry was music to her, his hands at her face a vise that delighted. As the whirl of sensations settled, she moved to put her arms around him . . . but the next thing she knew, Lynn felt the rug beneath her back as Reed guided her down, and then a pleasure so great it seemed as though the sky had split open and released all that was heavenly for her enjoyment alone. Now her fingers were in Reed's hair, clutching thick handfuls, while the rest of her soared, dipped, rose again to a place beyond all care. She knew she spoke, murmured, made sounds that sometimes were understandable, often not. She felt an iron bond with this man who loved her, who gave his love in gifts of ecstasy.

She was leaping, her body an arrow streaming fire, toward the sun. And the sun barreled closer, within reach. It was the brightest, most beautiful place. She grasped for it with every fiber . . . and found it, falling into it, consumed in shimmering flame.

Reed took her in his arms and held her tenderly against him. They dozed together on the rug, the drive along the water forgotten. Some time later Lynn woke, and after a minute Reed did also. Sleepily they made their way out and to her apartment, stopping often to hug. He was there in her arms and in her dreams all night.

CHAPTER EIGHT

Lynn hung up and walked around her kitchen, mulling the problem. Antal had a virus; Barrie had just said she'd been barely able to whisper into the phone. Labor Day weekend, the year's busiest, was only a week off. It seemed wise for Antal to stay home and shake the bug. But with business so good, the dining room needed an experienced hand in charge. Was there any way, Barrie had asked, that Lynn could hostess temporarily, without leaving Reed short in the kitchen? She herself could be an extra body in there, even with no skills.

It was nice to be needed, Lynn thought wryly. Even after all these weeks as a cook, she didn't feel like a functioning, contributing part of the system. She was usually too rattled for creative work, and the little she'd tried hadn't seemed to tap her talent. The dishes were perfunctorily good, but nothing to rave about. Not when she compared them to work she'd done in the past, when she wasn't under the gun.

It had been so long since she'd felt indispensable. She'd forgotten the sensation. Of course, she'd never loved hostessing, but there'd been satisfaction in knowing she was terrific at it. She missed the feeling of a job well done, the acknowledgment that a real void would open if she wasn't there to do it.

In fact, satisfaction wasn't something she had a lot of these days. She dropped into a chair and stared unhappily out the window. Another heat wave was smothering southern Maine; even the birds seemed enervated, going about their business in the maple tree less noisily than usual. About the only part of her life running on an oiled track was her relationship with Reed—and even there, hitches loomed. She adored him with a passion that at different times was ferocious, tender, and all shades in between. He was her lover, her friend, everything she hadn't known she craved. And the caring closeness that shaped their love was never stronger than when they were together in the private magical world desire made for them.

Out of each other's arms, though, they weren't as harmonious. She never doubted how he felt; the hours she spent in his embrace, the mutual giving, had shown her beyond question that Reed's emotions more than matched hers. She knew she was precious to him in the way she'd come to care. He gave back her respect and esteem. But with the gulf between her ways and his—and most crucial, the way he saw things happening next, versus the direction she wanted—well, sometimes she felt as close to him as if they were listening to different translators over earphones. And there was an icy knot in her stomach that was getting harder to ignore.

As much as Lynn wanted to pretend it wasn't, Gull

House was changing. She'd battled over the big things Reed wanted to do, but she'd looked the other way while more and more of his small ideas had taken root. Especially lately—probably to pacify him. Anything to keep the prospect of his buying in at bay.

He wasn't going to be put off forever, either. She could only mollify him for so long by letting him experiment and redo. And the effects of that were unnerving enough. The life she'd built for herself over the years, painstakingly insulated with layers of the sameness that spelled security, was being dismantled bit by bit.

Would he stay if she said no? When he'd made it clear how important it was for him to become more than an employee at Gull House? There weren't any answers. If she prevented him from buying in and he stayed anyway, to be with her, he'd resent being held back. If she relinquished part of— But that wasn't possible. She simply couldn't give in to the final invasion.

She rubbed her temples with her palms. All this tension and the morning had barely started. She was no closer than ever to solving that mess. And now there was a smaller but more immediate problem: poor Antal, and how to replace her. She willed the murkier matters away.

Could she do both, if she and Reed put in extra preparation time? If more dishes were ready to go, instead of being cooked to order, and Barrie lent a hand?

Say they got everything set for lunch that they could. Then she'd throw on a gown, play hostess, return to the kitchen to prepare for dinner, and change again. It would mean going in early, working madly through what was normally a comfy afternoon lull, and staying late—but it could be done.

She phoned Reed.

"There's a problem," she said when he answered. "Antal is sick, and we hope if she lays low she'll be all right for the weekend. We figured I could hostess if you and I get a head start on lunch and dinner. It'll mean I won't be in the kitchen after we start serving, but Barrie can give you some help. It should only be a couple of days, anyway. What do you think?"

She heard nothing but his faint breathing.

"Reed? Oh, no. I bet I woke you up."

"Yep."

She pushed away the picture in her suddenly fevered mind of his sleep-warmed body, strong and tanned. He'd probably kicked aside the sheet in the humid night, and he'd be naked, stretching, now reaching for his glasses . . .

"I hope it wasn't too much of a shock," she said.

"Could have been worse."

"Really? Good. Well, anyway—"

"You could have injected ice water intravenously."

"Oh. I'm sorry. I should have been more gentle."

"That's my line. So what you're saying is, I ought to get dressed and hustle my tail over there, right?"

"Right. If you don't mind working like mad for a couple of days . . ." She ran out of steam. Her plea was nervy under the circumstances, she realized. He wanted to be a part owner instead of an employee; she was asking him to act as if he had an investment in the place.

But his mind was speeding in another direction. "Will there be a bonus for this?" he asked huskily.

Her knees went custardy. That was his love voice, the one he used when they were completely alone and his lips were close to her ear. A kaleidoscope swirled past her mind's eye, images of the two of them together . . . here, in the stream, in her dressing room.

"I'll—" she began in a frog croak. She cleared her throat and started again. "I'll try to think of something."

"You do that," he whispered. "See you in a half hour."

It was nearly three when Lynn changed back into the jeans and shirt she was using for cooking. Her feet hurt. Her body craved the break she usually took between lunch and dinner. But she didn't dare linger in her dressing room. Too much to do.

She hurried downstairs, anxious to get into the kitchen unnoticed. The world wouldn't explode if the late lunch customers happened to catch their hostess dressed for house painting, but it would be unprofessional to be seen that way. Especially by this bunch. She hadn't worked the dining room in two months, and the crowd had changed more than she'd realized. The familiar sweatered ladies with gunmetal-colored hair were still there, the portly men in condolence-call suits—but where there was once just a sprinkling of the trendier types, now they equaled, if not outnumbered, the old customers. *If I see one more set of designer cotton separates, I'm going to pour cocktail sauce on them,* Lynn thought. It didn't seem to matter that she hadn't let Reed buy in. Gull House's reputation, its whole atmosphere, was new—and it was obviously his style that was making the difference.

She heard raucous laughter from the dining room and paused in the reception area. The table of eight she'd seated earlier, affluent thirtyish couples thin as fence posts, were now several drinks to the wind and yukking it up. She watched for a moment as they shrieked over a boating story someone was telling.

Other customers were glancing at them in annoyance. Lynn sighed. Hobo clothes or not, she'd have to nip this in the bud. She went to the table.

"Excuse me," she said. "I'll have to ask you to keep the noise down."

Eight razor-cut heads swiveled to look at her as if she'd just announced that the special of the day was creamed ashtrays.

"If you don't mind," she added with a polite smile designed to fool nobody.

She turned and headed for the kitchen. No one had seemed startled by her jeans. *Not that this crowd would notice if I wore a bear suit.* Well, at least she'd gotten a chance to pick off a few of the enemy.

She pushed open the swinging door and felt the tension curl in her stomach, as usual, when she walked into the kitchen. Funny; it hadn't been there when she was hostessing.

"Welcome back," Reed said. "I missed you. How'd it go?"

"Fine." She put on an apron. "Was Barrie able to do much?"

"She was great. Hacked up the lobsters for the salads and everything. She said she'd be back later. But I missed you."

Lynn's face got warm. "You said that already."

"I'll say something else. You looked incredible in that pink dress."

"Scarlet."

"Yes, Rhett darlin'?"

"Huh? Oh." She chuckled. "I mean the dress was scarlet. It must have looked pink in the fluorescent light."

"Well, it reminded me of how you looked back in June, when you wore those things and I kept wanting to—"

"Reed—"

"Oops." He glanced around at the few remaining kitchen workers. "They'll be leaving for their break in a couple of minutes. Anyway, I'm sure they didn't hear."

He pushed his hair back, and she saw the repaired earpiece on his glasses. She'd noticed a few days ago that he'd had it fixed, and she'd felt a pang. Idiotic, but there all the same. She was feeling less and less needed. Not by Gull House, not even to keep a stupid pair of glasses intact.

"What's bothering you?" he asked.

"It shows?"

"Does to me."

She shrugged. "Just anxious to get through this and have Antal back," she lied.

He glanced quickly at her but didn't say anything. He went back to his tiered vegetable and seafood mousse, his latest creation.

"That's so pretty. The colors," she said.

"Thanks. It's moving well too, better than I expected." He worked in silence for a few minutes. "You know, that means a lot from you. A while back, if I'd tried anything like this, you would have had my legs broken."

"You're exaggerating."

"Well, I—"

"Just the fingers. Of the left hand."

"Really, though, Lynn. I can see you're trying to be flexible, and I love you for it."

She didn't answer. How could she tell him that things like his lovely mousse—and the new people who were descending on Gull House in hordes to eat them—were causing a chill under her skin that worsened by the day . . . and that the only reason she made herself accept so many of his ideas was so he'd stop bothering her about buying part of Gull House?

"Know what else?" he asked.

"What?"

"Everybody's gone." He came up behind her and she felt his hands at her midriff. His lips pressed the tender skin of her temple and trailed down the side of her face. She lifted her head when he reached her chin, and a fluttery weakness washed over her as his mouth worked at the baby-soft flesh underneath.

He moved up and kissed her eyes, his tongue exploring the hollows by the bridge of her nose. She tried to get out of his hold to turn fully around and embrace him, but he kept her where she was, his hands firm.

Her head struggled to remind her that someone could walk into the kitchen at any time. *Just another minute, and then I'll . . .*

"I love you, Lynn," he whispered against her mouth, and then his hand was sliding beneath her jeans, pressing her belly, pushing her hard against him. She drew in her breath in a sharp gasp. *Just another . . .*

His lips were all over her face and neck, in her hair, nudging up her shirt sleeve to kiss her shoulder. Her hands tingled with wanting. There seemed nowhere to put them with Reed in back of her like that, so she reached up to hold his head where it was doing such lovely things. Her fingers weaved into his hair. She grasped the delicious thick silkiness of it. His splendid smell, a male-spicy-clean mix, surrounded her.

But she couldn't let herself be overcome. Someone was going to walk in any minute. "Reed," she said, her voice gritty, "we can't—"

"Shh," he said, and kissed her lips fully. She tried to pull away, but the hand still caressing her belly beneath her pants slid tantalizingly lower. If his tongue hadn't been filling her mouth, she would have cried out.

She sank back against the arms that cradled her. A

river of joy threatened to sweep away what fragments were left of her restraint. *Just another minute . . .*

Reed must have been fighting the same battle to contain himself. She felt a slow tensing of the muscles in his arms, and with a sigh of regret he removed his hand.

She hugged him quickly, tightly. If only they could do just this, love and hold each other all the time, keep the rest of the world and its complications away.

He bent and kissed her nose, leaving a dot of wetness. She made no move to rub it away.

"I didn't want to stop," he said.

"Neither did I."

"You didn't, did you?" He smiled lazily, love in his eyes, and reached for her again, but this time she had the clearheadedness to back away.

"Was that the . . . 'bonus' you had in mind?" she asked, turning back to her work space.

"It was a start."

She was groping for a suitable reply when he said, "Of course, only an employee needs to get a bonus."

It was a minute before she figured out what he meant. He hadn't said a word about buying in since they'd fought over the steamer. He knew her well. But she felt a pinprick of dread at the reminder of her dilemma, especially so soon after she'd delighted in the love and security of his arms.

Reed knew instantly from her silence what she felt, and he caught her eye and winked. She thought he was probably trying to make her see the remark as a lighthearted poke; he'd likely meant it that way. But she hadn't missed the flicker of a frown above the green eyes as his computer put the pieces together: if the topic made her uncomfortable, after she'd had two weeks to hash it over, she'd already made a decision—one he wasn't going to like.

"I haven't been up this late since I was born," Barrie said, and yawned cavernously. "What kind of tea do you want, Lynn? I have peppermint, chamomile, jasmine, lemon mist, and breath of goldenrod."

"What's breath of goldenrod?"

"It isn't. I just wanted to see if you were listening. You look as if you're going to fall asleep, cry, or implode."

"Is that why you invited me over?"

"Of course. Who would socialize at this hour, except in Transylvania? So. Peppermint, chamomile—"

"Chamomile."

"Good choice. Clean, natural, relaxing—"

"And put a slug of brandy in it."

"Even better." She left Lynn sprawled on the living room couch, put the water on, and came back. "Things went pretty well today, didn't they? We had to work our tails off, but we managed. I hope Antal makes it back soon, though. These late hours are murder. How do you stand it?"

"You get used to it."

"Okay. Enough polite conversation. You want to talk about it? And if you say 'About what?' I'll serve you your tea in your shoe."

Lynn rubbed her weary eyes. "Take it easy, will

you? No wonder you never became a psychologist. You'd have had the patients running away from you screaming."

Barrie dashed for the kettle, whose sirenlike wail was starting to rise. She returned with their cups. "I'll try to be less abrupt. If I just had a couple of crowbars to prop my eyelids up . . ."

"Shouldn't we whisper? I don't want to wake John."

"You won't. He falls instantly asleep at midnight and doesn't open an eye for anything less than a monsoon. Listen, are you going to tell me why you look so awful? What could possibly be the matter? You finally fall for a wonderful guy, and he seems nuts about you. Plus he cooks like a dream, he's got great ideas, business has never been anywhere near this good. So . . . ?"

Lynn sipped her tea and tried to let the hot liquid relax her. "I just . . . don't like it."

"You don't mean Reed."

"No. I love Reed." To the surprise of both of them, a fat tear rolled down Lynn's cheek. "I don't know what I'd do without him. I just feel so—unnecessary!" She wiped fiercely at her eyes. "It's so different now. Gull House, everything. What Reed and I have together is beautiful, but something's gone that I had before. I never know what to expect anymore."

Barrie's brow was ridged with concern. "But the restaurant—"

"The restaurant is a knockout! Business is booming!" Lynn punched the couch cushion. "All the old customers are still with us, and the BMW-and-beard types are trampling each other to get in. And he hasn't even been here three months!"

Barrie nodded slowly. "I think I get the picture."

"Can you see how it is?" Lynn implored. "I wish I was pleased that Gull House has a new lease on life, but I keep feeling worse and worse. All the years we worked on the place, like polishing a rock an inch at a time. And then Reed comes along, and bam! Diamonds overnight."

"So you're jealous."

"Yes. I hate it, but I am. He's taken something that was mine and run off with it, and all I can do is watch while he does better with it than I did. Before Reed came, you and I had a lovely restaurant that couldn't have survived without us. Now . . . I don't know about you, but . . ." Lynn's face worked as she tried to control herself. "I know what would happen if I dropped down a hole tomorrow! Nothing!"

"Lynn! How can you say that?"

"I can say it because it's a fact! Antal is a great hostess. No need for me there. And I'm about as essential in the kitchen as a third eyebrow. I've told you before—it just isn't working out in there. Anything creative I try, I have to leave in the middle because somebody sends back their bluefish. I'm always too busy to do any really nice cooking."

Barrie poured more tea. There was a worried look in her brown eyes. She sat on the couch, her small body nearly disappearing into the cushions. "I was hoping that would ease up."

"It hasn't. Reed gets better and better, and I just sort of stay where I am."

"And you haven't decided about selling him a share."

Lynn shook her head.

"Well, first of all, you're shortchanging yourself. Reed might have been doing fabulous things, but no way did he start from scratch. He walked into an established restaurant with a top reputation. And who was responsible for it? You, Lynn. You may be feeling like a fish out of water"—Lynn gave an unladylike snort—"but you get the credit for making the place what it is. The menu, the kitchen, were always your turf, and you know that's where a restaurant stands or falls."

Lynn waved the point away. "I know, but—"

"Take some confidence from that. Okay, you haven't hit your stride yet; perfectly natural when you switch hats. You need time. Listen to a true coward—I'd never have the guts to do what you did."

Lynn was quiet. Barrie had encapsulated what her own better judgment had been saying. But when judgment battled with emotions, it was so hard to—

"And if you don't want him to buy in, that's your business—but stop seeing every suggestion he makes as a threat."

Lynn's hands tightened on her mug. "Such as?"

"Such as expanding into the extra room. Business justifies it now. Weekends fill up a week in advance."

"I don't agree. After Labor Day we'll have an off season like any other."

"Of course there'll be the dropoff. But it shouldn't be as dramatic now, with the crowds we're getting."

"It's always significant. I'm sure we won't need extra space from fall through spring." Her sister lifted her blond brows in doubt. "Give me credit, will you please?" Lynn said. "My business judgment is fine. You're looking at me as if my brain hopped a bus to Salt Lake City and is never coming back."

Barrie yawned. "It's not that. I respect your opinion."

Lynn stood. "You're not tired or anything, are you?"

"Me? Nah."

They smiled at each other, wanly. Lynn knew enough to leave now; it was way past the time Barrie usually went to sleep. She could nod off in the middle of anything if it was late enough. "I'm going home before you fall on your face," Lynn said.

"It won't matter. I'm going to fall on my face anyhow."

Lynn heard the bedsprings before she had the door fully closed.

CHAPTER NINE

Antal was back, her usual high color dimmed, but well again. Lynn had welcomed her warmly, hiding her mixed feelings. Having the extralong days over with was a relief; changing from chef to hostess and back again twice daily had been a strain. But it had been gratifying too. The familiar mantle of the hostess job had brought a pride she missed terribly.

Labor Day weekend was nearly over. Sunday night—the vacationers would be heading home tomorrow. The local people showed the same attitude: back to work, play season over. Lynn knew from previous years that an invisible curtain was about to drop. Business would shrink abruptly in the next couple of days. But tonight would be busy—and a little crazy. It was like New Year's Eve. Hurry up and have fun, time's almost up. The spirit was infectious, and the nuttiness tended to spread to the staff.

I'll have to try not to catch it, Lynn thought, but she could feel the coil tightening in the kitchen, and she knew she'd be susceptible. She was unsettled enough as it was, with so many unresolved questions hanging in the air.

She finished arranging a bouillabaisse and set the steaming bowl for the waitress to collect. She stole a moment to admire the way all the clam and mussel shells pointed up, surrounding the mound of lobster pieces in the center.

"Don't bother doing it that way when we're this busy," Reed said. "It looks fine with the shells in a pile, and you can use the time for something else."

She started to answer, but remembered she hadn't added the garlic toast, and hurried to do that. Then she began on the next order—two easy broiled dishes, a Newburg, and flounder amandine.

A waitress shouted, "What happened to my three stuffed trouts?"

"Take it easy. I had to bone them," Reed said. "Here are two. Wait a minute and I'll have the other."

"What takes so long?" the waitress snapped.

Reed said, "Don't hassle me, we're up to our necks in here," and Lynn thought, *It's starting.*

She took her scrod and halibut out of the broiler, finished the other two dinners, and checked the next order.

"What's this second thing?" she asked Reed, showing him the slip. "I can't make it out. 'Bakswo'?"

"Baked swordfish," he said shortly, and tossed the slip vaguely in her direction. It missed, and he ignored it.

"Look," she said, picking it up, "this is a rough night for all of us. I wish you'd ease up."

"Me ease up? You're the one who's making extra

work for me. Are you going to learn to read soon, or will I have to keep interpreting for you?"

Lynn's eyes widened. "How much extra work is it to read two crummy words that I, not having your expertise in the professional kitchen, oh guru, couldn't decipher? I didn't ask you to sit down and read me *A Tale of Two Cities.*"

"Do me a favor. Don't ask me to do anything." He turned away and began throwing handfuls of crabmeat into a skillet. It was clear that he'd rather heave them at her.

Hurt anger roiling, Lynn went back to her work space. She prepared the swordfish, put it in the oven, and started on the rest of the order. *What is his problem?* she asked herself furiously, but she was very afraid she knew.

Finally it was past ten and the orders were dwindling. Lynn felt the tension slacken as the kitchen staff began to relax. They'd gotten through the weekend, and it was nearly over. She herself was still wound up, smarting from Reed's uncalled-for rudeness. She'd kept out of his way, and he'd left her alone.

"There're no more salmon croquettes," Lynn told Beth. "Let me know fast what they want instead, because we're starting to shut down."

Reed mumbled something, and Lynn said, "What?"

"Nothing."

He went back to what he was doing. She watched for a moment the ripple and flow of muscles in his shoulders and back while he put a shrimp dish together, reaching for his ingredients. There was a tight control to his movements. His whole posture, a kind of curled-in tautness, showed how on edge he was. As if she wouldn't have known from his outburst.

She swallowed and looked away. There was still plenty to do. She got busy fixing the rest of Beth's order.

"Okay," he said, turning to her, as if they'd been carrying on a conversation and she'd pressed him. "What I said was, we ought to shut down things like salmon croquettes for good."

"Do you think we could discuss restaurant policy later?" Lynn snapped back, and saw instantly, but too late, how she'd been baited.

"Do you think we can discuss it at all?" he demanded.

"Reed, this isn't the time or the place—"

"You're not going to let me in, are you?" he asked quietly, rage brimming in the soft menace of his tone.

She groped for a way to answer, to buy some time. But he took her hesitation for what it was, and the rigid lines of his face dissolved into fury.

"I should have known!" he shouted. "Why the hell did I waste my time being patient, waiting for you? You knew all along you wouldn't sell."

People were turning to see what the fuss was.

"Do you *mind?*" she said. "We'll have our differences out in private!"

"Our differences? No, Lynn. We are not talking about whether one of us hates tennis. My career and my future are at stake here, and I want to have it out *now!*"

Lynn's hands were clenched, her nails abrading her palms. Rage bubbled in her throat. All the smashed-down emotions of the past weeks were screaming for release, begging to be put into words and hurled at Reed. But she made one last effort to keep her dignity.

"Your career and your future," she said, spitting each word as though it were a nail, "will just have to wait another hour while we do our jobs in here!" She stomped back to her counter.

He followed right behind her, and she could almost feel the tangible force of his anger at her back when he yelled, "It's time to pull your head out of the sand and see what's really going on! You're a fool if you don't sell me a share! I've finally put some life in this place, and you want to turn it back into a morgue!"

The last string of her control snapped. She whirled to face him. "Is that the way you see it, the miracle worker reviving the corpse?" she screamed. "Your memory is as reliable as a stopped clock! You didn't walk into a flea-ridden diner and make it the flower of the Northeast. Gull House was a top restaurant while you were still flipping hamburgers for a living, and *we* made it that way! Barrie and I, us, me! Not you!"

"Well, you're damn lucky I came along when I did. How much longer do you think this antique was going to survive without some new ideas? If that's how you want to keep it, you'd better change the name to Dull House. You have no respect for anything the slightest bit different—"

"And *you* have no respect for anything that wasn't dreamed up by Reed Graham ten minutes ago!"

The other kitchen workers were openly watching, even the few who'd discreetly pretended not to hear at first. The machinery was loud, but the noisiest dishwasher, mixer, and food processor running simultaneously couldn't have covered the pitch their voices had hit.

He hurled a chunk of bluefish to the floor, and a cook jumped aside as it spattered. "Face it, Lynn. You need me. If it wasn't for me—"

"Oh, I need you, do I?" She grabbed a whole flounder, and was about to throw it at the bluefish when she realized that would simply lower her to his level. "Right. And I also need termites, hives, and a bad cold. Sure, things would be different if it wasn't for you! I wouldn't be breaking my back trying to please someone who isn't happy unless every single thing is done his way!"

"*My* way? For three months I've practically had to bring in bodyguards every time I wanted to change the least little—"

"*Yes,* your way!" She followed the direction of his eyes to her hand, which still held the flounder by its tail; it dangled wetly between them. She looked at it uncertainly for a moment, and then put it back on the counter with as much dignity as was possible under the circumstances. "You're hired by a fine restaurant whose cuisine has won prizes for years, and instead of compromising, nothing will satisfy you but—"

"Compromising?" He swept a pile of crab shells onto the floor. "*You* accuse *me* of not compromising? Lynn the unbendable, who watches to make sure I don't put five more parsley flakes than usual into the soup?"

"That's your faultless memory at work again. Step right up, folks, and watch the man rewrite history to suit his convenience. You were just telling me how flexible I've become! How much it"—she flung the word—"*means* to you! Well those days are over. It's time you learned you can't charm me into doing whatever you want. Gull House is my restaurant, and like it or not we're going to do things *my* way."

"I guess I can see how flexible you really are, huh, Lynn? You can't manage the tiniest little step, can you?" He was glaring as if she were a sickening variety of insect.

"If you mean letting you buy into Gull House—"

"Of course that's what I mean! What the hell are we talking about, hog futures?"

"We might as well be, if this is your idea of 'talking'! We could have had a dignified conversation in private, but no—nothing would do for the ego king but a public variety show, complete with flying fish!"

"And would it have made any difference? Are you going to pretend your mind hasn't been made up all along?"

"It hasn't!"

"Oh, give me a break," he said disgustedly, and turned his back. One foot slid on the wet floor, but he kept his balance. Lynn wished fervently that he'd fall on his face for the audience he'd barbed her into becoming a screaming maniac in front of.

But the steam seemed to have gone out of them

both. Lynn's wrath was replaced by embarrassment and sadness. No matter what corners of their relationship had poked into the public arena before, they'd never put it all out on display like this. And spats they'd had were just . . . spats. This was different. She didn't want to think about how different. Doing her best to ignore the curious and sympathetic glances around her, Lynn plunged back into work. Orders had piled up.

When she came up for air, it was after eleven. Only Reed and the two dishwashers were left. She wiped sweat from her cheeks, took off her apron, and left the steamy kitchen to wash up in her dressing room.

Wisps of hair were glued to her forehead and neck in wet curlicues. She swept them back with a cool washcloth, stopping to press it to her burning eyes. The emotional gauntlet she'd run tonight, plus the steam and smoke in the close kitchen, had taken their toll. She peeled off her sodden shirt and bra and put on a cotton blouse. As she reached for the light switch, her eyes went to the loveseat. The burning came again, this time from the prickle of tears. Reed on that black velvet when she made love to him . . . waves of passion's energy shimmered up from there, the afterimage of their love. She turned away quickly and left.

He stepped out of the darkness as she was approaching her car. She was all raw feeling; thought was suspended. There were no words. He put his arm around her and she rested her head on his shoulder. The damp night, so like that one in the pine woods, surrounded them with its perfume, the scents of summer's end.

Emotion ate at her like acid, a swirl of hot and cold sensations she couldn't begin to separate.

After a while he said, "I'll come home with you," and she nodded and got into her car. She drove to Sycamore Street and parked in her spot, and he pulled up behind her in the Dodge. He took her hand as they climbed the stairs to her apartment.

Inside, their arms went around each other and they held on tightly. Lynn's eyes stung again. She thought she heard the faint shudder of a sob as Reed drew in a deep breath. She snuggled her head deeper into the hollow of his shoulder and massaged his back, and he answered by gripping her tighter still.

He hadn't changed after work. His shirt was wet and his skin carried the scent of the kitchen plus his musky maleness. Lynn didn't mind. She let it fill her senses, blot out everything else, until she was intoxicated with it. Then she pulled out of his hold and began slowly to unbutton his shirt.

Reed took off his glasses and put them in his pocket. His hands went to her blouse. She looked up to find his eyes on her. The bare emotion in them was so intense, she stopped what she was doing, impaled; but then she had to look away, as if from a too-bright glow.

She ran her hands inside his shirt, over the damp chest, feeling the coarse hairs with their droplets of perspiration spring beneath her fingers. She laid her cheek on them, drinking in his scent again, and he clasped her head and held it there. There was a current in his hands, an electricity of caring that she could feel as surely as if his fingers were live wires.

He pushed her blouse aside and reached hungrily for her bare breasts. He held them with an urgency he didn't try to restrain, no slow teasing strokes to tantalize her. His hands went around her back and she raised her arms, expecting him to pull her near, eager to return the embrace; but he seemed to change his mind, not ready yet to relinquish the heated mounds. Cupping them, he lowered his head and took a nipple in his mouth. Sparks ignited a fuse that swept through her when his tongue moved. He flicked the point of it firmly back and forth across the sensitive bud, and the rough, wet sensation was galvanizing.

When he raised his head she moved close, pressing her breasts against him. Now it was impossible to know whether the wetness between her soft chest and his hairy one was his or hers. Desire was dampening Lynn's flesh as well.

They clung together, and Reed ran his hands down her back to her thighs, fitting her to him. He seemed to need her entire length against him. Lynn shifted in his arms to press tighter. Closer, closer still . . . she felt a primitive yen for the comfort of his body against hers, the balm of the emotion that flowed between them.

She could feel the reluctance in his arms when he released her, but it was only to gaze into her eyes again with that intensity that was like a charge. Lynn returned the look unflinchingly, all her feelings laid bare.

Without looking away, she touched his fly. He gasped and closed his eyes. She pressed, driven on by the rampant power under her hand. The pleasure in his face was nearly pain. A shiver racked his body. He pulled her to him fiercely and she arched her hips, an urgency mushrooming to answer his.

She wanted him wildly, so much she could have cried. She'd never been as full of tears as she was tonight. For now everything was arrowed in on her need for Reed, which had to be answered soon or she wouldn't be able to stand it. That was all she could handle for the present. Later she'd have to . . . but no. Not now. Blot it out, cover it, fill this empty ache with the lover in her arms.

He held her face. His breathing was heavy and uneven, and his hands trembled. He stared into her eyes for long seconds while gently wiping the sheen of perspiration from her cheeks with his thumbs.

It was the last gentle thing he did. His mouth came down on hers, and he thrust his tongue past her compliant lips. She tried to meet it, to welcome him and know the sensations she loved so, but he didn't stop for that. He'd traveled the contours of her mouth so often with soft, loving motions; now he was possessive, controlling. There was to be no meeting or sharing. She felt his tongue against the roof of her mouth, in the tender tissue of her cheeks. She felt it rubbing her teeth, and knew in dim puzzlement that it must hurt him.

Just as abruptly as he'd entered, he left her mouth. "Now," he said, and she nodded and moved eagerly with him into the bedroom. She reached for his belt, but he was removing it himself, fumbling as he tried to be quick.

She knew as soon as his shorts were off that she'd never seen him like that, the enormity of his need so evident. She moved toward him, wanting only to be under him on the bed. But his impatient hands at her waistband reminded her she was still half dressed, and she helped him take her pants off, her fingers working no better than his. She had a fleeting sweet recollection, with his touch on her waist, of that first night on the beach when they'd kissed. His hands then had been exquisite on her skin, knowing but tender. Now . . .

Now they were tumbling onto the bed. Reed was poised over her, not waiting for her to position herself; one leg dangled off the mattress. But it clearly didn't matter. He was going to take her where she was. He pushed his hands under her hips to raise her, and she stifled a gasp when he accidentally pinched the skin. Then he was entering, and she was ready, more ready than she'd ever been, but this time she did make noise, the pressure was so much. Where was the sweet rhythm that had become theirs alone, the perfect combining of two bodies in the thrill of love?

He heard her and paused for an instant, but then moaned deep in his throat and seemed to lose what thread of control he might still have had. He held her to him and plunged deep, deep, as though trying to reach her soul.

And after the first minute of fear Lynn was with him, traveling fast and hard. Now she understood his great urgency, the near-harshness of his movements, his supreme arousal. To be away was all that mattered tonight, to soar higher and higher until there was nothing but this, the ecstasy that transcended all rational thought and feeling.

Too quickly they were there, too far to hold back and remain together for longer than the lightning few seconds it took them to explode as one in a white-hot burst. Arms and legs locked in the desperation that was their love at this moment, they rolled over and over as the spasms ebbed, and finally were still.

They lay in the damp, twisted bedclothes, still joined. Speckles of weak light, the moon's glow diffused by the leaves outside the window, moved gently over them.

As Lynn came back to consciousness, the outside sounds of the night creatures reached her ears, reminding her of the lovely first night in her bed. She felt a rush of tears, but fought them back and snuggled closer to Reed. He held her tighter.

Minutes passed. Lynn drifted into a doze. She awoke to feel the deep regular breathing against her that meant Reed was sleeping, and closed her eyes again.

She didn't know how much time had gone by when, beneath wakefulness, she began to feel a pervasive warmth. Flame was licking along her limbs. Slowly the world returned, with its sad/happy truths: the thudding memory of last night's distress, and the awareness that Reed, who had never left her while they slept, was awake and moving within her.

Powerfully sweet it was, his big hands massaging her back while his lower body enticed hers into a slow and tender motion. Her fingers traced the hardness of his thighs, the rounded flesh of his buttocks.

The languid movement continued for long minutes. Their hands, moving in slow concert with their bodies, tracked each other's limbs, explored the sensitive flesh of inner arms, trailed along hips and backs. Occasionally the fingers met and clasped.

Lynn raised her leg and ran her toes down the back of Reed's calf. He responded by tangling his hand in her curls and pulling her face to his for a long, soft kiss. When it was done, they looked sleepily into each other's heavy-lidded eyes, their heads resting inches apart on the pillow, while still their bodies undulated together.

Reed began to stroke her face with infinite gentleness, over and over. His palm smoothed her hair, dampening again in the hot night, off her brow. He caressed her cheek, her ear and neck.

Lynn held his head and kissed him, gentle touches of her lips on his forehead, brows, and eyes. Her tongue flicked out to enjoy the tickle of his lashes. She moved down the night-stubbled cheeks to kiss the corners of his mouth. She opened her lips on the ridged bone of his chin and tasted him there, finding sweet-salty hardness. Like so much of the rest of him.

She laid her head on the pillow again and became aware that the tempo of their rhythm had changed. The gentle flow of sweetness through her veins was quickening, beginning to burn around the edges, as Reed's hips set a faster pace. She felt his breathing roughen and looked into his eyes, really looked—and could no longer deny what she saw there, what she knew he saw returned in her own.

Somewhere on a far precipice of her mind she'd known all along. Their love tonight, first with its consuming ferocity, and now with slow, sweet, infinite sadness, was a dance of sorrow, an exchange from soul to soul of what their minds found too painful to face.

She sobbed once, and Reed said, "Shhh," and kissed her mouth and eyes. His body seemed to be urging hers into one last mindless escape. In the wordless communication they'd shared from the very beginning, he knew she'd only now faced tonight for what it really was. He was trying to help her through it, help her find her own path of release as he'd found his in the hot, grabbing coupling she'd understood only vaguely, not ready then for the truth.

He eased her onto her back and began a deep, rolling motion. His torso was firm and knowing on hers, his hands caressing everywhere he could reach. Lynn's body moved, too, meeting his every thrust. But even as hot lightning flashed through her, even as the fire inside her flamed higher and higher with every stroke of Reed's vital maleness, scalding tears flowed down the sides of her face.

He licked them away, his breathing heavy in her ear. Lynn didn't try to stop them; she did nothing but move with him in the mounting cadence of their sharing. High enough, and the tears would stop . . . she'd be past this hurtful plane and transported into the realm she'd never known but with Reed.

They were nearly there now, joined in the climb to

the summit whose radiance transcended all concerns. Lynn felt Reed clutch her, and she held on tight. She wanted never to let go of him, nor of this rapture that bonded the two of them inseparably.

She was hazily aware that she shouted out, and that Reed did an instant later. Flame shot through her and from her, and she knew with the certainty born before humanity that the same wildfire was invading Reed, her love . . . her heartmate that she couldn't do without . . . and would have to.

She didn't know whether the tears had ever stopped, but they were there now, cascading to the pillow in a hot trickle of pain. And something else: they weren't only hers. Reed's face beside her was wet.

Through a hurting mist Lynn knew that some time passed—whether minutes or hours, she wasn't sure. But it was still dark when Reed left the bed and dressed. He moved about quietly, as if trying not to wake her, but Lynn knew he knew she wasn't asleep.

When he was finished, he sat on the bed.

"I have to go now," he said.

"Yes," she said.

"I guess I'll go to Boston, to my sister's."

She nodded, but he couldn't see in the darkness, and he said, "Lynn?"

"Yes, I heard you." She wiped her cheeks. "I love you."

"I love you too. But I don't . . . know what's going to happen."

His voice had cracked. It made her tears flow harder. *Stubborn fool! Tell him he can have his share!*

But that wasn't the answer. She knew as well as he did that mixing their careers, so vital to them both in their separate ways, was a fiasco; and the fact that their love transcended anything either of them had known wouldn't alter that.

She felt she should say more . . . but through the long night they'd already told each other all there was. No more words were necessary.

She felt him come toward her in the darkness. His lips touched hers in a kiss of such indescribable sweetness that she wished she could preserve it like a pressed corsage, to take out and savor during the days and nights without him that awaited. And then he left. He was out of the room and the front door had opened and closed in seconds. She pressed her face into the pillow and let the sobs come.

CHAPTER TEN

Barrie had done Lynn the kindness of telling the staff Reed had left, so she'd been spared that. But all week she'd had to bear sympathetic glances and oversolicitousness ("Can I carry that carton of milk for you?"). Everyone was watching her, feeling sorry for her. They wondered if Reed would be back, who would replace him if not, whether Lynn would run the kitchen herself, as she had all week.

Little do they know, Lynn thought as she rolled flounder fillets around salmon mousse, one of Reed's pushed-for menu items, *that I wish I had those answers myself.*

For now she could handle the job of head chef. She welcomed what little pressure there was; it distracted her. She could, in fact, head the kitchen alone right up till next season if she chose to. Even with the jump in summer business, the post-Labor Day slump had occurred just as Lynn had predicted.

But did she choose to? She didn't know.

Beth came into the kitchen. "Someone wants to know if she can have sea bass in herb butter instead of the gray sole that's on special."

"Sure," Lynn said listlessly. Her specials hadn't been very inspired this week. She'd have to work on that. If she felt like it.

She finished the stuffed flounder and started on the next order. Two baked scrod. Strange; even the orders were running in a more pedestrian vein now that Reed was gone. As if he'd gathered up and taken with him the innovative style that had gradually, even through her resistance, curled into every corner of Gull House, like a spirit. Involuntarily she glanced at the mostly unused sauté pans over the range. She recalled Reed's first night, the excitement she had felt as she worked the dining room, knowing he was in the kitchen and wondering when she'd see him. She'd balked at manufacturing a reason to go in. And then the problem had solved itself when—

"Are there bay *and* sea scallops tonight, Lynn?"

"Yes, but I only have about—let's see, two orders of bay. No more came in today."

"Save them for my table, will you? If it, uh, you know, wouldn't be too much trouble."

"Of course it won't," Lynn told the waitress, scowling, thinking, *Will you all stop treating me as if I had lost a leg?*

She returned to her memory. He'd asked Antal to send her in. She'd always remember that first sight of him, in his forest-green shirt, at the stove with Roger. So big and appealing, her heart had thudded like a pogo stick just looking at him . . . pushing the hair away from his glasses . . .

After work they'd walked on the beach. It had begun then, the ardent closeness that was to lead inexorably toward . . . Her face grew fevered as her memory made the jump from their kisses on the beach to the night of the flood—when at last the enticing tastes they'd had of each other had bloomed into the full expression of their caring. *Oh, Reed, I can feel you still.*

She willed her mind away from that dangerous territory. All she needed was the slightest hint of tears. One look at a reddening nose, and the waitresses would be ordering a wreath.

She thought back to last May, before Reed had come. There she'd been, a leggy dark-eyed brunette with hair a little too curly, mouth a little too caustic. Set in her tranquil ways. Working at a job that vaguely dissatisfied her in a restaurant she adored and was proud of. Avoiding romantic entanglements with the excuse that her work conflict took priority.

She arranged shrimp for scampi, tails up in a circle, and found herself adding a splash of brandy. The first time she'd seen Reed do that, she'd had apoplexy.

Now where was she? Still not happy with her work. Another job now, a different dissatisfaction, but essentially a step in place. Not seeming to belong anywhere. So battle-scarred from the affair she'd finally allowed herself that her nights now were purest hell. She slept, but not nearly enough, and it showed in her eyes and skin.

Was she better for it? In those unending nights she asked herself that often. *You could have stayed in the dining room, manless except for occasional dates, and your heart wouldn't hurt so now,* part of her would scold. In wiser moments she tried to look back on the summer and recall the rapture of her time with Reed with more pleasure than regret. She congratulated herself for having the courage to take that chance, and to risk cooking as well. Yes, she could have stayed in the dining room, and maintained her guarded life-style—and been bored and snappish, and angry at her inertia.

But mostly what ate at her at night were the memories of what she'd treasured. The delight of just being together. The provocative intellect, the creativity that was uniquely Reed's . . . that led him to recognize a like spirit, and cherish the qualities she'd always wanted a man to see. The wonderful fun, laughing together, their senses of humor so on target. The smell she could drown in, the arms and lips, the body she adored and that gave and took from her with delirious abandon.

It would be a long time before blessed forgetfulness would let her sleep past the keepsake remembrances, the soul's recollection of bliss now denied.

"Going home?" Lynn asked Barrie as her sister came into the kitchen from the dining room. "Nice jacket."

"Thanks. I just got it yesterday. Adds a little pizzazz to the jeans, don't you think?" She turned so Lynn could see the back of the red wool blazer.

"It's lovely. I wish it wasn't wool weather so soon, though. Two weeks past Labor Day, and I'm already turning on the electric blanket as soon as I get home at night."

Their glances met, and Lynn thought, *Uh-oh,* and Barrie asked hopefully, "It is getting easier, isn't it?"

"Definitely. Now some mornings I even remember to get dressed before I leave the house."

"Well, at least you haven't lost your sense of humor."

Yes, I have.

Barrie went on, "Don't push yourself into deciding about the chef job. Whatever you do is okay. Stay with it if you want, or we'll get someone."

If you don't stop being so bloody nice to me, I'm going to stomp on your petite foot.

"That place in Wells Beach is closing, you know, so that's one available chef. Or we could always . . ."

She kept talking, but Lynn wasn't listening. Discussing who might replace Reed made his absence seem that much more final, permanent. She turned back to the counter so Barrie couldn't see her face, but she seemed to catch on. She said good-bye and left.

Lynn worked for a while alone in the big kitchen. She was growing tired of having only her memories for company. But the cooks were due back for dinner preparations, and the waitresses would be in a bit later. Maybe this would be a nice, busy Sunday. She could remember when hectic dinnertimes had made her tense and irritable. No more; now she welcomed the activity. The harder the work, the better. Her mood lightened the most when there was so much going on that she had no time for anything but the here and now.

"Hi," she greeted Beth. "Got an order already? I guess it'll be busy tonight."

"With a Red Sox game on, and them fighting the Yankees for first place? Not a chance."

Lynn groaned inwardly.

"Listen, could you do a take-out?" Beth asked, dipping soup. "These are some of my regulars, and her sister is home sick. They want to bring her a crabmeat salad after they've finished."

"Sure," Lynn said. Good; she could take her time with that, keep her fingers working. In fact, she might as well start it now. Then she'd be sure to have it ready when they left, even if she was interrupted for more early orders.

She got out one of the aluminum containers they used as doggie bags. It was a shame to put a nice salad in an ordinary thing like this fluted silver Frisbee. She found some doilies in back of a cabinet and used them to line it.

Then she sliced tomatoes thin and arranged them with snow peas, standing upright around the rim of the dish. Inside the row of red rounds and green spikes she set leaf lettuce, letting its curly edges peek up over where the mound of salad would go.

As she diced the crabmeat, she glanced with pride at the waiting container. *I can take my sweet time doing this and be as finicky as I want,* she thought, *so there.* Since Reed had left, every magazine she'd seen had an article on getting over a breakup. At first she'd tossed them down, not wanting the reminder, but finally she'd read a piece, just to see. Among its tips had been one about using anger. Remember what he did that you loathed, it advised. And have a ball doing what *you* like that made him mad or uncomfortable.

Well, Reed sure would have hated what she was doing now. He didn't believe in spending extra time on the appearance of food. She'd always felt eye appeal was essential, and she enjoyed creating it. But Reed was basically right: there had never been time to squander in the bustling kitchen during the season.

She debated whether to whip up a homemade mayonnaise in the blender, and decided that would be taking her campaign too far. Things could get busy any moment now. She mixed the salad, spooned it onto the lettuce. She topped it with red and green pepper rings and feathery sprigs of dill.

Are you finished playing now? she asked herself, and answered, *No, not quite.* She sprinkled paprika inside the green ring, then minced parsley in the red one. *Now I'm finished.* With professional pride, she covered it and set it in the refrigerator.

The pace did pick up then, and when Beth came in an hour later to get the salad, Lynn had forgotten about it.

"This is gorgeous," Beth said, admiring it through the plastic lid. "It looks like it came from a caterer."

"Samson, or Samuels. I know it was something like that," Lynn said impatiently into the phone. "He fixed the back porch after one of the steps broke when we moved a dishwasher in, remember? And then he and his wife had a party, and he showed us the den he'd converted from a garage. But I can't find his number, even in the Yellow Pages."

"That's because his name is McNicholas," Barrie said, her voice thick with sleep. "Abner McNicholas. Why did you think . . . ? Oh, I know. His wife is Delilah. You're not going to call him now, are you?"

"Do you think it's too early?"

"Lynn, it's not even seven yet!"

"Well, I want to catch him before he leaves the house, so he can come today."

"Is it worth waking him up? If he can't come today, he'll come tomorrow."

"No! I have to make sure it can work the way I have it designed before I, uh . . ."

"Before you try to reach Reed."

"Yes. I don't want to go halfway and get everything in motion, and then find out it can't be done for some reason."

"But why do you have to move right this second?"

"Can't you see? Because I don't know whether he's deciding . . . whether he even still wants to . . . I just can't wait, that's all."

"Extending the pipes a ways for a sink and dishwasher, that's no problem. And some rewiring, and ducting for the oven, is all." Abner McNicholas looked around the wing of Gull House that was piled with extra chairs, booster seats, and outmoded appliances. "No problem. A week, maybe ten days."

"And breaking through for an outside entrance? You can do that too?" Lynn asked.

"Yep. You want a written estimate?" He dug into his Windbreaker for a pen.

"No, the price sounds fine," Barrie said. "Just go ahead."

"No, not yet," Lynn said.

Abner looked from one to the other.

"I'll call you later today," Lynn said.

Abner shrugged. "Whatever you say."

"Hello, I'm trying to reach Jill Edwards?"

"This is Jill Edwards."

"Jill Graham Edwards?"

"Yes."

"My name is Lynn Blackburn. You won't know who I am, but—"

"I certainly do know who you are, Lynn. I've been hearing your name constantly for two weeks! I'm afraid you missed Reed, though. He left last night."

"For home?"

"I think so."

She dialed with a shaking finger. Two rings, three. Four.

"Hello?"

"Reed!" She'd wanted to sound cool and cheery, but his name came out in a half choke.

"Lynn? I've been trying you all morning. Either the line was busy or there was no answer. I was just going to come over."

The beloved voice rumbled deliciously in her ear. He was going to come over! Then he must still—oh, but maybe he was coming to tell her—

"Reed," she began again, "I hope you were coming to—"

"Lynn, listen. I hate this. I haven't slept a whole night in two weeks. I want to be with you so much, I can't—see, I decided what I'm going to do. I'm going to invest in another place, some cuisine that won't compete with Gull House. Cambodian, anything. I'll have my piece of a business, and you'll still have your own, and then I want to get married."

"Married?"

"Married."

"But you don't have to—"

"I *want* to. Don't you?"

"No, I mean you don't have to—"

"No?"

"No, that's not the no I mean. We can—"

"I'm coming over now," he said, and hung up.

She ran to the window and opened it, opened the screen, too, and leaned way out. When she saw the Dodge turn into Sycamore, she raced down the stairs and out the walk, past a startled Mr. Petrie clipping the hedge. Reed saw her and lurched to a halt. Without pausing to park or cut the ignition, he leaped out and grabbed Lynn in a hug so tight it knocked the breath from her.

"Are you going to marry me or not?" he pleaded.

"Yes! Yes! But I had to tell you—"

"Thank God," he whispered, and buried his face in her hair.

Oh, she thought, *the smell and feel of him, so wonderful . . .*

"I want us to be together for good, that's number one. And I'll get my own restaurant, and if you're not happy cooking or hostessing at Gull House, I'll help you find what you like," he said into her neck.

"But I found it," Lynn said, laughing with joy. She told him about the catering business she'd be opening in two weeks at Gull House.

"It's all planned. I was up the whole night mapping it out. The contractor came this morning, and he'll start on the wing as soon as I call him. And Reed"—she pulled away to see his face—"that means you don't have to buy in anywhere else. Do it here. You'll run your kitchen, and I'll run mine."

"You mean that?"

"I sure do. I finally realized that it wasn't Gull House I couldn't bear to give up—it was the illusion that I still had a function in it as it was. I couldn't face the fact that I'd outgrown what I was doing and I'd have to break new ground to be happy. So the present kitchen will be your turf. I'll have my own."

"A whole new kitchen's going in there?"

"Yes. And I'll be able to cook the way that's natural for me—at my pace, with time for arranging and presenting. I'll take only the jobs I really want. I can't wait!"

"Well, nobody could do better with a venture like

that than you. It's a perfect idea. I'm so proud of you, Lynn."

His lips found hers, and once again, after so many endless, aching nights with only remembrances for warmth, Lynn knew the dazzle of tastes she loved, the sweet union of their mouths.

Suddenly she remembered where they were, the public front yard with Mr. Petrie outside. She broke away, embarrassed, to find the white-haired man gone and the clipping shears on the ground. But then she saw Reed grin widely, and she turned to find Mr. Petrie there with Reed's car keys.

"Turned off your engine," he said, handing them to Reed. "Couldn't help overhearin'. Maybe after you get married and get a little used to seein' each other, you'll stop leavin' cars in the street wastin' gas." He winked and went back to the hedge.

Public yard or not, Lynn couldn't stay away, and her arms went up around Reed's neck as their lips met in jubilation.